Horse Laughs and Hard Knocks

Jim Nelson

Lone Pine Publishing

The Publisher: Lone Pine Publishing

10145 – 81 Ave.	1901 Raymond Ave. SW, Suite C
Edmonton, AB T6E 1W9	Renton, WA 98055
Canada	USA

Website: http://www.lonepinepublishing.com

Nelson, Jim, 1949–
Horse laughs and hard knocks

ISBN 1-55105-245-8

 I. Title.
PS8577.E378H67 2000   C813'.6   C00-910672-3
PR9199.3.N358H67 2000

Editorial Director: Nancy Foulds
Editorial: Erin McCloskey, Dawn Loewen
Production Manager: Jody Reekie
Cover Design: Robert Wiedemann
Book Design & Production: Heather Markham
Illustrations: Tim Heimdal

Cover Photo: Mark and Leslie Degner, Wilderness Light

We acknowledge the financial support of the Government of Canada through the
Book Publishing Industry Development Program (BPIDP) for our publishing
activities.

PC: P6

Dedicated to the memory of

James Fonger,

who, for me, epitomized

the true Western Gentleman.

Acknowledgements

These stories are, for the most part, based on actual horses, people and events. Any resemblance, therefore, to anyone living or dead, could be more than coincidental. I have changed many of the names because I have found most students of what I refer to as the "School of Horses" to be rather humble about the lessons learned there.

However, there are names like Doc Somerville, Jonas H. Webber and Midnight, which have been etched in the annals of the school in such a way that there is no getting around them. But I am not a historian. In "The Mare's Secret," for instance, I have laid out the bones of the story much as I heard Jonas, and others, relate it. While it would be interesting to dig up the actual court record, etc., it is the story that interested me. Neither have I attempted to contact the Dahl family, who owned the horse, to get their side of it. I feel that that story, the whole story if you will, is theirs to tell. For my part, I am satisfied that any horse that came out of the chutes in the 1930s, and is still the subject of controversy today, deserves mention. To paraphrase the great Will Rogers, "all I know is what I hear around the campfire."

Most of the stories, of course, take place much closer to the here and now, and I have been either a participant in, or an eye witness to, the events that inspired them. But it takes a lot of horses to make a book like this, and I confess I have been forced to borrow some of them from people like Murray Sutherland and the Foster Brothers.

I must acknowledge my brother, Don Nelson, who inducted me into the School of Horses some years ago and from whom I have stolen more than one of these tales outright.

Finally, I must say that without the ongoing support and indulgence of Lynne Ness, the book would never have been written.

Thank you all.

Contents

The School
of Horses

*N*ow, there is one thing you always want to remember about the School of Horses, and that is that when it really gets down to it, the people involved don't matter. Of course, you may receive the odd relevant word through people—horses don't talk—but the lesson itself always comes directly from the horse.

An example comes to mind from my own personal experience that illustrates this perfectly. It is a case where, in any other school, the teaching would have been done by the elder, myself, and the learning by the younger, my teenage nephew Kirk. But as it was, and as it always is in the School of Horses, we took turns being the students and the horses did the teaching.

I can't say that I qualify as any sort of equine professor anyway, although I have been hangin' around the corrals long enough to know better. And the kid, well, kids aren't supposed to know anything anyway.

6

It was still winter out at the ranch, and, feeling a little inflated after one of those Sunday dinners my sister-in-law is famous for, I had stepped out for a stroll. I had in mind a kind of a half-baked notion of catching up an old saddle horse for a leisurely digestive ride in the crisp evening air.

As I drew near the corrals, I noticed that Kirk seemed to have a similar idea. He was just drawing up the cinch on a horse I didn't know, a young Fjord gelding. A further glance around the corral revealed its perfect match in a mare tied to a post a short distance away. The Fjords are a sort of sawed-off, all-purpose workhorse of Scandinavian origin, with a reputation for strength, versatility and quiet temperament.

A few idle moments of chatter exchanged between the boy and myself revealed that he had taken upon himself the job of breaking this pair of lineback buckskins to ride, pack and drive. He looked forward, upon completion of the task, to sharing in the profits of his work when the pair sold as a "broke team" at the upcoming spring sale.

About the time he had buckled the double rigging in place and let his hands wander in a last-minute check over the cinch and up to the bridle, he had also discerned my notion of going for a lazy ride.

"Well, take this one," he said, the opportune nature of the moment apparently occurring to him as he spoke. "I gotta ride the mare too," he added, thereby explaining that by taking this saddled and waiting gelding off his hands, I'd actually be doing him a favour.

"What's he like?" I asked, removing the toothpick from my teeth and regarding the horse sceptically.

"Slow," said the seventeen-year-old with a note of disgust that could have been aimed at the horse but that I felt had been aimed at my superfluous caution.

The buckskin stood squarely on all four feet in the sleeping position and stared into oblivion completely unaware, or at least uncaring, of the prospects. I gathered up the reins, which hung loosely from his neck.

"I meant," I said with my own note of disgust concerning Kirk's confusion, "how's the breaking goin'?"

"Oh," said Kirk casually. "Fine, these Fjords ain't exactly hot-blooded." Again his tone seemed barbed with the suggestion that I might actually be shrinking from the prospect of climbing aboard this wanna-be plough horse. To dispel this notion once and for all, I began making ready to do just that while further clarifying the question.

"I mean," I said with a slight impatience I hoped was not lost on the boy, "have you been able to teach him anything?"

"Well, he don't neck rein at all," he confessed humbly, "but he'll 'gee-haw' fine."

I lifted my left foot into the stirrup, eyeing the sleeping horse.

"And he don't bite er kick." Kirk continued as I began lifting my considerable weight into the saddle. My right leg was well on its way in search of the right stirrup when, with scarcely a twitch of the ears, the horse erupted as if out of chute number nine!

The first buck left me sitting astride not the saddle but the rump, which served as a launching pad at the next buck. I soared into the air, lazily turning one hundred and eighty degrees before landing hard at Kirk's feet on the frozen floor of the corral.

"And, he bucks a little," the kid said through the grin escaping his previously inscrutable face.

By the time I had picked myself up the horse had settled down again. He looked back at the two of us as if curious to see what his exertions had accomplished.

"And he bucks a little?!" I demanded of the smirking nephew.

"Well, not every time," he said with a shrug, which turned out to be the case as I climbed aboard the second time. In fact, he performed pretty much as Kirk had initially led me to believe he would as we took a controlled turn of the home quarter.

Back at the corral the mare had turned in a similar, well-controlled performance, whereupon the young horse trainer decided it was time to hook the pair to the wagon. Now there are a variety of approved methods of breaking a team to drive, and depending on the terrain, the skill of the teamster and the horses themselves, Kirk's idea would qualify. I had my reservations, and voiced them, but to no effect. Kirk was feeling the pride of his natural strength hardened by the outdoor life of the ranch. It was he who had dropped the first loop over the heads of these buckskins. He'd taken them through halter training to driving them in the harness. He had driven them one at a time, then both together, until walking behind he could bring them to a polite stop with a voice command and a firm tug on the reins.

All this, I began to fear, had given Kirk the illusion that his own physical strength was sufficient to actually halt this ton-and-a-half of horse flesh whatever the circumstances. I mumbled a few suggested precautions, all of which fell upon deaf ears as Kirk made ready the pole and double-tree on the wagon.

"Do you know," I said, "if you're bent on this we could run a sort of jerk line from one bit back through the other on the inside rings, and I could ride with you just in case you end up with a runaway—I wouldn't touch it unless you called for it."

"No, that's all right," he said, polite enough but leaving no doubt in my mind that he needed no help in the worry-wart department. On the other hand, it was clear that he wouldn't mind if somebody held the horses' heads while he carefully and quietly hooked the tugs and climbed up into the box to take up the reins. This being done, he gathered up the slack and nodded.

The School of Horses is in many ways the perfect place for young people to gain a rudimentary knowledge of their own strengths and abilities. It showed in the confident grip upon the reins, and it glowed in the eager eyes as the voice casually intoned, "Git up."

The horses' ears twitched. One horse took a cautious step forward, and the second horse followed. The tugs began to tighten but neither the mare nor the gelding seemed bothered by the weight. It wasn't until the wagon actually began to move that the team took particular notice of it.

In fact, it was at precisely this point that the animals seemed to agree unanimously that whatever this lumbering thing was pounding and jerking along in pursuit, it was not to be trusted and the best thing to do would be to outrun it, which of course, proved difficult as they were securely attached to it by the harness chains.

In three jumps it was an all-out runaway between the banks of ice-encrusted snow lining the driveway leading to the main road. Kirk was finding that even with both heels hooked into the wagon box and pulling back with all his might on the reins, while screaming the appropriate voice command, the team simply ran on all the harder.

Looking ahead to the right-angle turn where the driveway met the road, he was struck by a clever notion to edge the outfit into one of the snowbanks in an effort to slow it down. Unfortunately, the steel rim of the wagon wheel cutting through the ice-encrusted bank brought the wagon to a complete, if momentary, stop, whereupon it rear-ended the horses.

Kirk seemed to carry on indecisively for a time, dragging between the wagon and the plunging team before finally relaxing onto the ice, whereupon the empty wagon neatly ran over his legs. The team went on to roll the wagon at the end of the driveway, and then continued on to the neighbours, where they caused all sorts of nervous speculation as to the general state of things up our way.

The responsibility for the next day's events (after retrieving the horses, wagon and sundry bits and pieces along the way) remained Kirk's.

"I didn't tell 'im to hook that team," was all his father had to offer by way of summing things up.

Pride aside, along with gruesomely skinned-up hands and face, and bruised legs that sort of knocked together as he limped from one horse to the next, the boy's injuries hadn't really amounted to anything compared to the ominous responsibility of breaking the team. That now meant undoing what he had inadvertently accomplished with the runaway.

Kirk's father had taught him that "horses do their learning by repetition or severity." There was little doubt, owing to the severity of the previous day's lesson, that when hooked to the wagon, they would tend to perform the same tricks again. Gone was the boastful confidence that had been growing in hard-won and totally legitimate victories over past days. Gone was the lust for battle that was replaced now with a mournful resignation to what seemed a sorry fate.

Limping sourly along behind them in the corral, the kid found the team unspoiled to any of the lessons gained there. It was the wagon they feared. It was the wagon that he had, inadvertently, conditioned them to react to by running away. It was the wagon that he would have to pilot in such a way that no one—not himself, the neighbours nor the horses themselves—need fear it.

But how? Plowing through the fields still buried in crusted snow, he ran the risk of balking them. This was the cardinal sin of breaking a team to drive. Something about offering a young horse a load that it could not or would not pull could somehow break the unwritten contract between teamster and team and render a horse useless to the purpose for the rest of its life.

"We could try that jerk line," I said absent-mindedly, in the same moment wondering what had induced me to offer to sign on for such a hare-brained, hair-raising ride.

Hope rose momentarily in the boy's eyes only to be deflated by practical considerations, followed by a shrug of resignation. "Why not," he said, rising painfully. I felt that his tone did not bode well for our chances.

Sure enough, three jumps into it, we were aboard a runaway. I stood braced behind the kid, waiting for the sign that I should try my jerk line.

"Yes! Pull it! Pull it!"—"you idiot" strongly implied—as he had apparently forgotten we had this card left to play before hitting the end of the driveway.

I reeled in the line hand over hand, effectively banging the horses' heads together and throwing their weight in the hindquarters to the outside. Their line of vision was thrown almost at each other, and while still trying to run, they were thrown off stride.

This seemed to give Kirk just enough of an opening to get their attention on the reins where he could impress upon them the lessons won back at the corral. When they slowed up, I let up. When they charged the bit, I checked them again.

"I love that thing, I love that thing," Kirk gleefully proclaimed as repeatedly we came to the brink only to back off in control again.

By the time we ran out of driveway, the horses were beginning to learn that the wagon was not actually going to eat them tail-first as it rolled and banged along the frozen road. Between Kirk and myself, the lessons learned would make quite a tally, but no one ever graduates, in fact only a fool would ever pretend to be a graduate, from the School of Horses.

The Horse Cab

*F*ar from having strict entrance requirements, it is possible to enter the School of Horses without fully realizing it. Such was the case with Beady Bob and the two boys, aged eight and eleven, who innocently signed up the man for a crash course from the school.

His name was actually Robert Foster, but folks had long since reduced it to Bob and added Beady because he wore them—beads that is—around his neck and wrists and wherever else it suited him. Beady Bob was what some people refer to as an aging hippie—a not entirely unfair description given his appearance and general lifestyle.

He worked at odd jobs, travelling from one to the next in an elderly Volkswagen bus. He bothered no one, and if his tobacco smelled a little green from time to time, or if he seemed to have little or nothing to do some days, this was made up for with the often-heard comment, "but he's got a good heart."

In fact, it was this very soft-heartedness (the more unchari-
table would say soft-headedness) that got him into the School of
Horses.

* ⋆ *

The Effingtons, in particular Wally Effington, had contracted
Beady Bob to make a sign for the gatepost at the end of their
driveway. "Effington Acres" was to be identified in rustic lettering on rough-hewn tamarack and slung from a wrought-iron
frame bolted through the enormous spruce post (complete with
extravagant burls). Bob had already spent more time barking,
sanding, drilling and varnishing the post than would seem prof-
itable, given what Effington had deemed the contract to be
worth—but time was not money to Beady Bob. He had spent
even more time preparing the tamarack slabs for the words. He
used a variety of hot iron bars to make it look like the lettering
had been done with a branding iron. At last, the sign was done
and needed only to be fitted into the wrought-iron frame now
swinging from the post.

To accomplish this, Bob had backed the old Volkswagen bus
in alongside the post and climbed atop its roof. He was barely
able to reach the sign, which he had leaned up against the bus,
but was doing his best to haul it up after him when he was joined
by the Effington boys.

"Ya need a hand?" said Pat, the elder boy.

"Well, I just might at that," said Bob. "Watch yerself," he continued, as the boys leapt to the task.

Young Pete's end of the sign sagged a little as "Effington
Acres" was slowly lifted beyond the boys' reach and disappeared
over the edge of the roof.

"Can we come up there?" Pete called out. Bob's head reappeared. He gazed down at the freckled faces, their eyes gazing
expectantly up from beneath their mops of curly red hair.

Following his natural disinclination to deny anybody anything, Bob acquiesced, though once up on the roof he did disap-
point the boys a little by making them sit down.

The Volkswagen rocked pleasantly as Beady Bob hoisted the sign into the iron frame and bolted it securely. The boys offered their frank appreciation of the creation. Bob had to admit that he was himself impressed with the finished product and sat down cross-legged beside the boys to take in its full effect.

"This is sure a big van," said Pat.

"Real big," said Pete, cautiously peeping groundward. Beady Bob was gazing contentedly at "Effington Acres."

"It's bigger'n a horse," Pat said, sizing up the general dimensions of the roof.

"A lot bigger," said Pete, still looking down over the side.

"We got a horse," said Pat matter-of-factly.

"But we don't got it here," said Pete sourly.

Bob became vaguely aware that he had missed something as he glanced from his personal reveries into the meaningful stares of the two pairs of eyes beside him on the roof of the bus. "What's that?" he asked.

"We got a horse but he ain't here," Pat explained.

"Ah…," said Bob, still feeling as though the pitch had been thrown before he reached the plate. "Where is he?" he asked, attempting to take up the thread.

"Just down the road, across the creek in Jenson's pasture," stated Pat. "We can't ride him home across the bridge."

"Our dad said," Pete added with a note of finality.

"He bought him for us when school got out and he's gonna haul him home—but Dad's never here." Pat's tone implied a tragic injustice in the thing, along with a sense of urgency.

"Summer holidays is almost gone," Pete added, and his chin slumped sadly onto his knees, which were drawn up against his chest.

"Well," said Bob, uncomfortably aware that the two were obviously losing heart, "I'm sure he'll be getting around to it soon."

Pat looked at him ironically. "He's bin going to do that sign since before Pete was born, our mom says."

"Yah," chimed in Pete, "before I was born."

"Well, he's a busy man," Bob stated, but his heart did not share the sentiment.

"You could haul 'im for us," Pete broke in.

"I could?" Bob was genuinely surprised by the idea.

"In this here van!" The younger Effington pointed emphatically to the object they were seated upon, his eyes flashing to life.

"It ain't even ten miles, and we could gas ya up if ya don't mind purple." Pat's offer came a little too quickly, betraying premeditation in an idea that up until now had seemed happenstance.

"You want me to haul your horse in this?" Bob asked in amazement.

"What else can we do?" Pete's frank summation left Bob momentarily without a clue as to what else "they" could do.

"But how would we get a horse into a VW?" Bob's question was not intended to be argumentative, nor was Pat's answer.

"He'll just go in!" he said, authoritatively adding, "We might have to take out a little of the stuff, but you can pick it up when we get back."

Bob looked at the two young horsemen. He pondered a moment, then gave a shrug. "Well, I suppose we could try it," he said.

The boys scrambed down off the roof and began dragging out whatever tools and accessories they deemed to be in the way. Pat dispatched Pete for a bucket of oats and a halter shank, and the trio were on their way before Bob had quite caught up with himself.

⋆ ⋆ ⋆

The boys sat on the edge of their bucket seat jointly pointing the way. The gravel road dipped dramatically in a sharp curve before hitting the approach to the bridge over the creek. Climbing the curves on the other side, the air-cooled motor slowed to a sputter before Bob offered it a lower gear. At the top of the climb the road straightened out again, and in minutes Jenson's pasture lay before them.

Sure enough, there among the cows lazily chewing their cud stood the lone horse. Its dapple-grey coat stood out against the tawny green of the ripening pasture. It seemed to take no particular notice of their approach as the boys bounded ahead of Bob, who ambled along, hands in his pockets.

"He's part Arab!" Pat said proudly.

"An' part something else," Pete added importantly.

The animal barely raised an ear as the younger Effington wrapped his arms around its neck in a loving hug.

Only when Pat shoved the oat pail up around its nose did the "part Arabian" show any real sign of interest. It muzzled a mouthful and began munching contentedly—not unlike the cows, thought Bob, which gazed at them stupidly.

"C'mon Silver," Pat said authoritatively, then remembered the shank, which he snapped onto the old leather halter. He took a step or two, gently tugging on the shank, but it was not until he gave the oat pail a shake that Silver picked up his ears, and his feet, and commenced a slow plodding march in pursuit of the pail.

The Volkswagen bus was parked on the road in the direction of home, its side door open to the pasture. Bob held the gate open for the plodding procession composed of Pat, walking backwards, pail in hand; Silver next, eyes, ears and nose fixed on the oats; and Pete bringing up the rear.

At the bus, Pat stepped up into its cavernous depths, tantalizingly shaking the pail as he did so. Silver's head and neck followed, stretching as far into the vehicle as possible, but his feet remained on the gravel, inches from the threshold. Even his lips seemed to stretch as the boy held the oats at whisker's length.

"C'mon boy, you can do it," he said, teasing the horse with the tiniest of nibbles.

"Push him!" Pat barked at the two onlookers, and Pete and Bob as one gave Silver a mighty shove in the rear. Over-balanced as he was, the horse nearly fell flat on his face, but gathered and lunged, depositing both front feet amidships upon the metal floor of the VW. Pat darted deftly out of the way between the two bucket seats, coaxing all the harder as he did. For a moment, the horse seemed doubtful, almost embarrassed, by the awkward posture and novel surroundings he found himself in.

He began to turn his head, but as he did, Pat corralled his nose with the oat bucket, and as the lips began to twitch after the elusive treat the boy hollered, "Push 'im again!" They did, and Silver's hind legs and tail clambered on in the bulging bus. Bob, getting into the spirit of the thing, shot the sliding door shut as Pat, finding himself backed hard against the windshield, squirmed off to the passenger side still managing to hold the comforting oat bucket aloft. Silver, still adjusting his stance, continued to fill his cheeks.

The horse was slobbering oats and looking curiously down the road through the windshield when Pete and Bob came timidly forward to survey the results of their joint efforts. Silver stood straight, his withers bulging into the tin roof of the VW. His tail hung down over the engine compartment in the rear, and his front feet were planted a step behind the two bucket seats. His neck and head, which of course he couldn't raise beyond the height of his shoulders, protruded between the driver's area and the passengers'. It seemed, at least for the moment, that a horse did fit into a VW bus.

"Get in!" Pat yelled at the two curious faces while holding the oat pail within easy reach of the horse's slobbering lips. They leapt into action—Pete shoving in beside Pat and Bob sliding into the driver's seat. Silver gave no particular notice as the engine sparked to life. Neither did he seem particularly interested as Bob eased the bus into motion down the gravel road. Bob, on the other hand, did take note of the extra half-ton load that his novel passenger represented.

The VW took its time gaining momentum. The shift into second gear caused the horse to lurch slightly as he adjusted his balance, but did not distract him from the oat bucket Pat valiantly maintained within easy reach. By the time Bob shifted into third, the bus was already approaching the winding downhill run to the creek.

Approaching the first turn, Bob eased off on the gas only to find that the bus continued to accelerate as a result of its weighty load. Coming into the turn, the driver was moved to gently apply the brakes, sending Silver into a short tap dance on the metal floor of the bus. This would have been fine but for the fact that it wasn't enough and the VW continued to pick up speed as it whined around the first turn and dove into the next.

Bob gave the brakes a more insistent shove just as the road curved from right to left, making Silver's job, standing upright, all the more challenging. For balance, the horse immediately threw his head in the air, except that there was no air, only the tin roof of the VW that sounded off loudly as the road continued to spin by at an ever-increasing rate.

"Slow down!" the boys screamed in unison. They may have been speaking for Silver as well, who was having great difficulty concentrating on the oat bucket as he danced this way and that, and forward and back, with each new application of the brakes.

"I can't slow down!" Bob yelled back over the sounds of the spraying gravel, the whining engine, the dancing hooves and the head banging into the roof. Having nowhere to back up to, Silver began crowding forward. When a further abrupt application of the brakes brought him nose to glass against the windshield, the horse began exploring—first the driver's side where he was brushed off by Bob, then the boys' side where there was little room between them for a horse's head, much less a horse.

It became obvious that Silver was deciding to bail.

"Get back!" Pat yelled, and Pete crawled under him for cover. The animal turned again to Bob and began crowding into the driver with some force. With his free hand, although he really didn't have a free hand, Bob began pushing back the horse's face just as they hit the bridge approach. At the speed they were now travelling, it could be said that they ramped the bridge approach. For a brief moment, all were suspended in air, experiencing that feeling of weightlessness that thrills rollercoaster riders.

But it did not thrill the riders of the VW bus, least of all the horse. When they came down, the weight of the load caused a sort of trampoline effect—Volkswagens do not have a rigid frame. Silver, who had probably never been suspended in the air except by his own efforts, seemed to find the experience totally disagreeable. This, and the fact that he seemed to be experiencing a wave of claustrophobia, brought on a sudden and dramatic change of temperament in the usually placid "children's horse."

Laying back his ears, Silver began kicking to the rear while almost simultaneously baring his sloping yellow teeth and nipping at those he obviously felt to be responsible for his predicament. His fellow passengers responded with screams and wild swings at the horse's head.

The good news was that on the other side of the little bridge the road was uphill. The bad news was that as Silver began to bite and buck, the bouncing effect was doubled, causing both front doors to suddenly pop open. This in turn brought on even greater screams from the boys caught between the passing gravel and the flashing teeth while Bob had the wheel to hang on to.

The bus had not coasted to a stop by any means before the boys opted flat out for the gravel, leaving Bob to his own devices. Silver continued in all-out revolt. Beating the horse off with one hand, Bob was somehow able to steer the bus long enough to yank the parking brake before effecting his own exit onto the gravel. Although the bus ground quickly to a halt, it continued rocking violently as Silver kicked and tore at every corner in search of the escape hatch.

Deciding whether they really wanted to release this horror into their midst, the cringing trio hesitated before snapping into action.

"Let him out!" the boys screamed at Bob, who flew to the side door and threw it wide as he and the boys retreated a respectful distance. No sooner had the light dawned in the open doorway than Silver burst through it head first, effecting a sort of somersault that none of the witnesses present could later quite reconstruct.

Once out, the horse seemed to shake off the rage that had transformed him into such a terror. This, much to the relief of his two owners and Bob, who had been ready to climb a nearby tree upon the animal's release.

The boys, at first humbled by the apparent failure of their plan—to say nothing of a newborn fear and respect of their faithful steed—soon took heart in the animal's apparent return to "normal." In fact, with one last shuddering look back at the bus, the "part Arabian/part something else" began plucking up the knee-deep grass surrounding him in the ditch.

They were across the creek! The boys suddenly realized they could ride home from here.

Pat tied the halter shank back to the halter on the off-side, thus effecting a crude set of reins. He then ordered a leg-up from Bob, who approached with residual caution, still smarting from the nips he had received. But the horse barely stopped munching while Pat slipped aboard and Pete scrambled up behind.

Then, with the boys' legs thundering along his sides, Silver ambled along the ditch up the hill to Effington Acres.

As always, there were a variety of lessons for Beady Bob to ponder as he idled along behind. The first, he supposed, might be: do not haul horses in Volkswagen buses. But lessons won in the School of Horses inevitably go well beyond such mundane details. As Beady Bob watched the boys prodding and scolding their steed for its frequent snack breaks, he had a vague sensation of having been part of a good thing.

The Doppler Effect

*V*ictoria Mulaney-Mablethorpe, Commercial and Residential Real Estate Agent was preoccupied with her name. When she had married an aspiring young attorney, the handle had seemed to lend an air of sophistication to her business card. When she had divorced five years later, she had not wanted to bring further attention to the fact by changing her business name as well. But in the year that followed, "Ms. Mulaney-Mablethorpe" had come to feel grotesquely large somehow—perhaps all those *M*s. She had never been a Vicky, certainly not a Vic, so most people asked for her by her full name.

Perhaps that was one of the reasons she got on well with Bud Fix. Bud, of indeterminate age, a roustabout who made his living working with other people's horses, called her "Miss M&M"—Em for short. He was due to arrive this Saturday morning to commence work on her latest prize, a five-year-old Hanoverian stallion.

In the divorce, she had kept the house and barns and the surrounding forty acres—the lawyer got the rest of the quarter—and they had no children. Dependants, however, had included Barney and Betty, a registered Quarterhorse gelding and Thoroughbred mare, respectively. Their papers showed their ages to be "getting up there." Their grass bellies showed the fact that they seldom worked.

Victoria had been active in dressage and a little show jumping before the marriage. With her interest in horses rekindled, she failed to find satisfaction in the rides offered by her two old friends. Scouring the markets and market trends, she had eventually landed the Hanoverian stud at "a steal" for five thousand. But that was before breaking costs. Still, she could not fail to make her money back on the offspring of the new stud and the older Thoroughbred mare. Unfortunately, so far the two had not taken much of a liking to each other, and that worried Victoria Mulaney-Mablethorpe.

Bud smoked—and his truck smoked. Bud suffered from indigestion occasionally; his truck only that morning had been suffering from a touch of water in the gas. Such were the ruminations of Bud Fix as he cruised over the gravel road. It had never before struck him how much he had in common with his pickup—although he did stop short of talking to it. That was the trouble with a pickup truck as opposed to a horse: a horse listens. On a long trail, typically in bad weather, Bud would ride along sharing his political theories, psychological observations, even personal intimacies, and the horse listened carefully to every word and never argued or breached a confidence. Talking to whatever machine you happened to be keeping company with, you knew you were talking to yourself.

Perhaps that was why Bud appeared, in some people's eyes, to neglect his vehicle. A search through the box of the truck would reveal a wide variety of items, many of them thought to be lost. Nestled in last winter's hay and twine was a large inventory of ropes, tack and tools, empty beer cans, shotgun shells and a dead coyote that Bud had never quite got around to skinning. It was not disdain Bud felt for machines so much as indifference. As long as the windshield wasn't too cracked to shield the wind, as long as the pistons went up and down and the wheels went round, it served its purpose. It seemed foolish to Bud that anyone would think of giving their vehicle a weekly bath.

The one thing you would not have found in Bud's truck box even if you dug all the way down to the rusty wheel wrench—which Bud did—was a spare tire. His jack-all was at home holding up the tongue of his horse trailer. He'd stopped for coffee, of course, and come out to find that a tire had gone flat. He'd borrowed a jack, rolled the tire down to the garage to be fixed and gone back to the café for another coffee.

Bud Fix was a slow movin' man and well used to a variety of self-imposed alterations to the course of the day—Victoria Mulaney-Mablethorpe was not. "Well, Miss M&M," Bud drawled as he emerged from the pickup. Victoria held up a hand, signalling the importance of the phone call she was engaged in. She sat upon the top step of the modern ranch-style home, the cordless hand-set held to her ear, a look of deep concentration etched upon her brow. Beside her on the step was an empty coffee cup and beside that an expensive and stylish riding helmet. She was attired in white jodhpurs, complete with leather inserts, an equally white turtleneck and black riding boots that came to her knees.

"Tell them that there may possibly be some sort of blind option, but be sure they know that we have to move fast. They can't sit around on this one if they want to scoop the receiver general…that's right, and call me back." As she lowered the phone, her simmering gaze rose to meet Bud's affable appraisal.

"You're late," she said curtly.

"Oh?" said Bud, sounding a little surprised if not dubious. "I don't know if I'd call it late," he considered. "I believe there's daylight enough to make a day out of it yet."

"Ten-thirty, Fix," she read from the face of her electronic daytimer before snapping it shut and setting it beside the phone on the step. "It is now almost noon."

"Was I holdin' ya up?" Bud asked, sounding more curious than apologetic though certainly considerate.

"No, you weren't holding me up," Victoria said, rising abruptly, "but The Prince is furious." She strode towards him, automatically gathering up the phone and daytimer as she moved off the step.

"The Prince," Bud echoed rather blankly, "is what?"

"I've had him penned up in the corral since ten in case you actually came a bit early—that's a laugh." She swept by him with the air of a foreman kicking a sluggish crew into action. Bud fell in behind.

"The Prince? That's what you call this new cayuse?" Bud asked.

"It's not what *I* call him, it's his name—Prince Doppler. And for five grand he is no cayuse either, I'll have you know."

"Course not," Bud mumbled. "I just meant, well, that's quite a handle for any horse."

"The Prince is not just any horse—you better get used to that fact before we go another step." She stopped abruptly. Bud almost walked into her. She stood with her arms folded, tapping one foot impatiently, her eyes fixed in the general direction of the barnyard and corrals that had just come into view. Following her gaze, Bud discovered a black horse about seventeen hands, smooth and sleek with a full mane and tail.

The animal was agitated, it was true, but from the way he paused to hold his nose into the air then skipped into a trot squealing back at the offending breeze, Bud surmised that his late arrival was not the source of the stallion's impatience.

"We may have to move that mare downwind," Bud pondered aloud.

"Ha! He's not interested in her," Victoria snorted. "I had them penned together for a week and they didn't so much as rub noses."

"Well, something's rubbin' his nose today," Bud mumbled thoughtfully.

The phone rang. "Yes!" Victoria snapped into the flip-out mouthpiece. "Yes, this is she," she continued. Her eyes went blank as she began rattling off numbers and words in a language foreign to Bud's ear. He sauntered on down to the corral to lean his elbows on the top rail. The Prince offered him one brief sidelong glance before once again skipping into the hurried trot, head high, nostrils flaring.

"Carries himself well," Bud muttered. "Er tries to…," he added thoughtfully.

Bud ducked through the rails and sauntered into the corral. He extracted a cigarette from an inside pocket, struck a wooden match on the zipper of his fly and squatted on his heels in the middle of the corral. Exhaling smoke from both nostrils as his concentrated gaze followed the horse back and forth from one end of the corral to the other, Bud seemed genuinely interested. The horse seemed oblivious to all but the wind and the four white planks barring his way.

"There's no way he's going to settle down now," Victoria said, a look of real concern pervading her features from the far side of the corral.

"Is there someplace we can put that mare?" Bud asked matter-of-factly.

"It's not the mare," Ms. Mulaney-Mablethorpe answered impatiently. "He gets like this when he's cooped up for too long; he gets bored."

"Well, I think I can keep him amused if I can get his attention—but I can't compete with the come-on he's gettin' from that old Thoroughbred floozy of yours."

"She doesn't even know he's alive," Victoria protested.

"She'll know it when he finally decides to jump these rails," Bud said. He took another lazy drag on the cigarette, still following the stallion's movements with his eyes. "And so will that gelding," he added, thinking out loud.

"As if he could jump this fence," Victoria snorted impatiently.

"He can, and he will as soon as he lays eyes on 'er—he's a jumpin' horse, ain't he?"

"A show jumper, not a fence jumper." Victoria seemed indignant.

"He'll be jumpin' everything in sight once he claps eyes on that mare." Bud seemed mildly amused by the prospect as he continued to meditate on the stud's movements.

"I'm telling you—" Victoria snapped.

"Humour me," Bud drawled, discarding the cigarette as he rose, still eyeing the big black horse, and strode towards the woman. He vaulted the rails. Landing lightly outside the corral, he walked past Victoria, disappearing into the open door of the small hip-roofed barn painted fire-engine red with white trim. A second or two later he reappeared, halter shank in hand, and stepping through the small picket gate into the pasture made his way directly towards the mare and gelding standing on the far east side.

"I'm telling you—" Victoria began, but the phone rang. "Call me back," she barked into the machine, snapping it shut and striding out after the man with the rope. "I'm telling you, it's just because he's been cooped up!"

"It's the east wind," Bud responded. "Hardly ever blows from where she's standing back to the barn and corrals—an' then maybe when it has, she just ain't come around." At this point, Bud slowed and took a bead a few degrees off the mare's nose. He began talking to the animal softly. "Hey girl…whoa now…"

"I live with these horses and I'm telling you Betty here has nothing like what you're describing on her mind." The brisk walking seemed to take some of the absoluteness out of Ms. Mulaney-Mablethorpe.

"It's just that," Bud said quietly as he began stroking the mare's neck, "when I get holding hands," he was now working the rope around her neck, "with Prince Dope—er whatever…"

"Doppler!" Victoria interjected, startling the mare briefly. "As in the Doppler effect—speeding faster than sound?"

"Yeah, well, Prince whatever, but when I get holding his foot up I don't want Miss Betty here to suddenly get interested and walk into the picture."

By this time, he was leading the mare, and Victoria, to a lone spruce tree on the far west side of the pasture. "I'm paying you to break The Prince, not to hold his hand."

"Yeah, well that's another story," Bud said, now stopped at the tree, "but one thing at a time." He moved to tie the halter shank but Victoria stayed him with a hand on his arm.

"That won't be necessary."

Bud seemed momentarily at a loss.

"She is trained to stand," Victoria continued authoritatively.

"But wouldn't we have to stand with 'er?" Bud asked, sincerely curious.

"No, of course not, where would the advantage be in teaching her to stand if you had to stand too?"

"Well," Bud said, pushing back his Stetson and scratching his head.

"Betty!" Victoria commanded while standing near the mare's head. "Stand!" she said, releasing the halter as she did so. "Stand!" she repeated once more and backed away, turning sharply to escort Bud away triumphantly. "There, you can stop worrying about the poor old mare and get on, finally, to what you're supposed to be doing here."

But Bud, turning to look back at the mare, standing obediently under the tree, seemed not quite clear.

"You mean she's just gonna stand there without even moving her head?"

"Exactly," Victoria answered.

"Well, then she wouldn't even notice the rope," Bud protested weakly.

"C'mon," Victoria said, and once again turned Bud towards the barn and his appointed task.

⋆

The Prince was standing on the far side of the corral. As the man and woman came into view around the corner of the barn, he gave barely a flicker of acknowledgement. His long mane and tail moved slightly on the breeze as the horse relaxed, his head down slightly, one foreleg bent in the sun.

"He's calmed down a little seems like," Bud observed.

"Whatever, get on with the breaking." Victoria was adamant.

"Well, I can't do that either exactly, I—"

"Why not this time!?" Victoria was getting exasperated.

"Well," Bud said, lighting up another smoke, "because he's already broke, for one thing." He put one boot up on the rails and leaned his elbows onto the gate like he was going to talk for a while. "And then that right foreleg, that he's got crooked up in the sun like that, it's hurtin' 'im—not now standing there like that, but it hurts him to step on it hard like when he's running or carrying somebody on his back."

Victoria Mulaney-Mablethorpe seemed momentarily at a loss for words.

"Course he ain't five," Bud went on, "more like seven or eight, I say eight, but we can look in his mouth."

"What do you mean, he's broke?" Victoria seemed to be struggling.

"Well, he's broke—he may be a bit spoiled, or quite a lot spoiled, but he's broke—fact is he's probably done some jumpin'."

"Why in the wild and woolly would somebody sell a horse as not broke when it was broke?" Victoria, one could see, was about to demand that sense be made of it all.

"Well...," Bud pondered. "I s'pose if he was broke you'd quite naturally want a demonstration, which would naturally bring attention to that leg—as it was, they were probably doping him a little anyway just for the ring."

"He was sold sound." Victoria was ready to take action.

"You're right, to your eye he was sold sound—they'd only say you did it to 'im since you got 'im home, er loadin' 'im even—there ain't no 'guaranteed sound' in horses, really."

"Really!" fumed Victoria.

"Course, I ain't sayin' he's unsound permanently. I'll have to look at it, but my guess is that he's pulled a tendon or something. It only hurts 'im to work it and then not that bad—rest it and he could be sound as a dollar in a few months."

"A few months!" Victoria was aghast.

"Course he can still cover that mare of yours. I just wouldn't ride 'im till you're sure that he's healed—it'd just hold him back."

"How…you don't know any of this—you've never seen this horse before and you haven't laid a hand on him!"

"Well, I could show you some, but…"

"Yes," snapped Victoria, "I think you should. Just go ahead and show me!"

With a shrug the man lifted the latch on the gate and strode confidently, patiently almost, towards the horse. By the time Victoria had closed the gate behind herself and caught up, Bud was standing at Prince Doppler's head, running his right hand down the horse's neck while, with his other hand, patting the horse's deep chest. His hands never stopped moving as he began talking quietly, repeatedly, almost like a chant. "Sun feels pretty good on that leg, eh boy? Eh Prince? Eh Doper?"

"Doppler," Victoria interjected, but quietly. Instinctively she had drawn up a few paces back. The horse responded with a lazy yawn. This the man took as a sign that he could begin exploring the leg in question. His firm strokes almost like a massage over the shoulder became lighter, acutely sensitive to any sensitivities the horse might have as the one hand worked its way down the leg. The hand on the chest seemed to hold the animal steady as Bud discovered a vein of discomfort and the leg stiffened.

"Easy there, easy now…" A look of deep concentration became etched in Bud's expression as he alternated comforting strokes with more discomforting explorations. At last he seemed satisfied. The horse relaxed once again.

"No big deal, eh boy?" Bud's expression relaxed as he addressed the woman standing behind him in the same quiet confident tones while continuing to handle The Prince.

"Could even be just a badly bruised muscle, maybe a few weeks'll take care of it—in any case we'll keep a watch on it, but I don't think there's much to fret about."

"And?" said Victoria Mulaney-Mablethorpe as if Bud had been making a sales pitch.

"Oh…," Bud said as he straightened his back. He tipped his Stetson forward over his eyes as he scratched the back of his head, then removed the hat altogether and ran his free hand through his mat of unruly hair. "…the breaking?" Bud still hadn't looked away from the horse. "Well, you can see the saddle marks as well as I can."

Victoria glanced at the small flecks of white hair where a saddle ring or latigo had scarred the black coat.

"That doesn't say how they made out," Victoria said in a slightly taunting tone.

Bud glanced into the sleepy eyes of the big horse. "Should we show 'er, Dopey ol' boy?" he said. He stepped back alongside the horse and still talking to him placed a hand on his withers and the other on the broad black back. With one final glance at his head and a "Whoa, boy, whoa!" Bud vaulted belly first onto the back, then rolled a leg over while pushing himself into a sitting position never once taking his eyes off the horse's head.

Then, with both hands on his hips and a careless shrug, Bud turned his eyes mischievously on Victoria.

"Was there anything else?" he asked.

"Mhhh!" was all she answered, and she didn't have a chance to say more for in the next instant the stallion lifted his head with a snort and bolted. Bud had just enough time to snatch a handful of mane as the big horse leapt along the rails, nose in the air. Victoria, seemingly invisible to the stud, only had time to leap out of his way as he wheeled and charged across the corral. As he sailed over the gate, Bud had two hands clamped onto the mane as well as both heels into the horse's ribs.

Betty, the old Thoroughbred mare, apparently decided to mosey up and see if she was still required to "stand." She now waited for news in plain view, not far beyond the pasture gate, which Prince Doppler cleared with even greater ease as Bud surveyed his own prospects.

There are, according to the Breeder's Handbook, many places a handler does not want to be while the stud mounts the mare, and sitting bareback atop the stud is one of them.

Bud had no choice as far as he could see. Bailing off at this speed didn't seem to be much of an option—until the old gelding, getting into the spirit of things, came looming into view off to Bud's right. The mare was running to Bud's left and a bit ahead when the stud's ears came back and it took a sharp dodge at the gelding.

The gelding hadn't quite gathered the significance of the stampede or the bared teeth and so was a little slow in veering off. The stud, on the other hand, was distracted enough by the mare still running on ahead to spare the gelding a grim explanation, and in so doing provided Bud with the split second he needed to execute the only plan that had occurred to him since the proceedings began.

As the stallion forged past the somewhat confused old gelding, Bud, affecting a move not unlike that of the bulldogger in the rodeo arena, lunged at the gelding's head. In the next few seconds Bud hung by one arm clamped in a chokehold around the gelding's neck and his other hand locked onto its leather halter. His feet dangling below slowly touched down in jolts and skips like a plane landing on crutches.

The gelding, completely confused by now, had no apparent desire to carry on in this mad stampede and pulled up in fairly short order, whereupon Bud landed both feet firmly onto solid ground.

He wasted no time in jerking the horse around and leading it back towards the corral, keeping one eye over his shoulder for the stud. Arriving back at the gate and Victoria, who for once was speechless, Bud drawled, "You did want the stud turned out with the mare?" He then added in a more serious tone, "Keep this old boy away from 'im or The Prince there will stomp his last few remaining years right out of him."

Bud then advanced the view that it must be getting on towards coffee time and Victoria, for once, agreed with him. In fact, Victoria Mulaney-Mablethorpe seemed to have relatively little to say as they made and drank coffee. What was there to say, really, that hadn't already been said?

"He's a jumper, Em," Bud reflected.

"Yes, he is, isn't he," Victoria said, and seemed to brighten at this undeniable fact.

The Mare's Secret

Old Swede instructed me to pound two big nails halfway into the first post, one on each side, near the top, in the direction the new rails would run. He then ambled off on old Bender, shaking out a loop as he went.

By the time I had the two nails sticking out of the stout tamarack corral post, they were back. Swede hunched over slightly and kind of crooked to one side as he rolled a smoke; Bender bobbed along at his steady even pace while pulling another tamarack rail along behind him.

With the odd lazy glance behind as he lit his freshly rolled cigarette, Swede guided the horse into a line that brought the rail to a stop before the post I'd just put the nails into.

Bender went into reverse as the man on his back gave the rope a flip that sent it round the post, trailing under one nail and over the other. As the horse continued in reverse, the slack in the rope came taut and the heavy rail slowly levitated into place.

"Nail 'er," Swede said in the act of crossing his left leg over Bender's neck and settling in comfortably.

The work settled into a productive pace. I was kept busy nailing, bucking the ends off with a swede saw and tending to Swede's rope as we'd change ends on a rail.

Swede would sit gazing over the brood mares in the next corral, pointing out the flaws in this one and that and challenging me to remember a single colt that had ever inherited, directly, one of those defects.

"Poor mare can throw a perfect colt," he'd say, and pass on to the next example.

I had pointed out that a swede saw worked better with a man on each end of it, but Swede had informed me that this was largely myth for a swede saw the size I was using. As a favour, he instructed me on the proper one-man use of the tool. "Let the saw do the work," he'd say, like a coach on the sidelines. "Don't lean on it; let the saw do the work." There is really no arguing with a man named Swede on the subject of swede saws.

I worked on steadily while Bender and his bent old rider kept a fresh supply of rails hoisted into place.

"Ya know, they say a horse don't think!" Swede said, gazing off across the mares. "They say they don't have feelin's like you er me."

"Who says?" I asked him.

"Who says what?" Swede barked as if I was a distraction.

"Who says 'a horse don't think?'" I quoted him back.

"They do. Those experts; the guys who write the books." Swede was getting impatient. "They'd say, fer instance, that this old nag a' mine couldn't pick me out of a line-up of one 'nless I happened to be carryin' an oat bucket, er a whip, er whatever they're used to—they'd say it's the bucket not the handler they'd recognize!"

Not knowing whether to agree or disagree at this point, I finished sinking a nail into the tamarack and asked, simply: "So what?"

Taking the stale butt out of his mouth, Swede stared at me with the cold blue bloodshot eyes of a chain-smoking hawk.

"Did ya ever hear a' the Halcourt Doll?" he asked.

"Some, I guess," I responded.

"Now are ya gonna tell me that horse didn't think?" Swede looked down on me from old Bender as if it was perfectly all right for me to be stupid, expected even, as long as I didn't persist in my stupidity beyond Swede's obvious and enlightening proofs.

The fact is, I had not previously formed a firm opinion on either side of this apparently common debate, but I had heard of the Doll. "She was some kind of killer buckin' horse back in the dirty thirties, wasn't she?"

"Well," said Swede, re-lighting his stub of a cigarette, "no, she wasn't. She was quite the other way; in fact little children rode her bareback to school two and three at a time with a loop a' binder twine around her neck. Them kids were crawlin' over and under her and fallin' off and fightin' over 'er, and she never pawed a-one of 'em!"

Swede took a long and significant drag on the butt that was out and went on without noticing.

"And yes! She was a buckin' horse, as great a buckin' horse as ever lived—and that includes the great Midnight! I knew a man," Swede paused for effect, and to give the butt one last roll around the premises, "maybe the only man in the country who could say he tried 'em both, an' he said the Doll was as great a buckin' horse as ever lived—yes! She was a buckin' horse…in the rodeo arena…and a polite 'n gentle member a' the Doll family, back on the homestead."

Swede didn't look at me as he began coiling up his rope and Bender kicked into gear on his way for another rail.

"An' she never thought a damn thing about it," Swede mumbled as he rode by, "accordin' to the experts."

I went back to sawing and nailing and thinking about the Doll. I remembered hearing the stories of her famous dual personality—but there was more to it, details I couldn't quite place.

* * *

When the next rail was up I decided to ask Swede what he thought the Doll was thinking—if only because I'd get to take a breather if he talked long enough.

"What she thought drivin' cowboys into the ground, er what she thought at home playin' with the kids?" Swede asked.

"Either one," I said, sitting on the rail I'd just nailed into place.

"It don't matter what she was thinkin'," Swede responded, with "ya damn fool" strongly implied. "The question is, if horses don't think or have feelin's fer...things, then how in the hell could she keep pullin' the switch without a slip-up?" Swede and Bender went back to work again, so I went back to work again, and by and by I took a slightly different tack.

"It seems to me I remember something happened to that horse, didn't it?" I asked Swede.

"A' course somethin' happened to 'er," he began. "She become her own rodeo event, fifty bucks to anybody who could turn in a qualified ride on the Doll—and fifty bucks was a fortune and a half back in them years!"

"But nobody was good enough to claim it," I volunteered.

"This is where that fella I mentioned comes in. Jonas Webber rode 'er—in fact, they carried 'im outa the arena on their shoulders throwin' their hats in the air—but there was more to it 'n that," Swede said with a sad and knowing look, as he gathered up Bender and his rope and we went back to work. After a while, I tried prompting him again.

"I keep thinking there was something odd about the Doll's story, but I can't quite place what it was."

"Well, fer one thing," Swede said, spitting out an unwelcome strand of tobacco, "Jonas never got his fifty bucks!" He paused, adding to the suspense. "By the time all the hoopla settled down and he made it up to the pay window, the judges had reversed their decision sayin' he pulled leather!"

"That's right," I said, recalling the scandal. "He took them to court, didn't he?"

"Fer all the good it did 'im." Swede said in disgust. "The stands were full a' witnesses, if he'd pulled leather somebody besides a crooked judge er two woulda seen it."

"So what was the deal there?" I asked.

"The deal was the mare," Swede said. "She'd bin sold to a rodeo contractor from down south—the man paid big money for a horse that had 'never bin rode' and that's the way he wanted to keep it. Nobody but the judges knew how much it cost the fella, but I imagine it was more'n the prize money."

Swede and Bender ambled off as I dredged the details of the court case out of my memory. The judge had decided in Jonas' favour concerning the ride and the money that he was owed, but he also ruled that community associations were a limited liability situation and as such couldn't be made to pay up.

"I knew there was something odd about that story," I told Swede.

"Business is business, that ain't the odd part." Swede seemed indignant.

"What do you mean?" I asked, straightening my back and wiping the sweat from my forehead.

"Ya gotta ask yourself," Swede leaned forward in a conspiratorial manner, "ain't it quite a coincidence that she should end up gettin' rode the day she gets sold?" Swede raised his eyebrows and dropped them with a knowing nod, but I wasn't getting it and probably looked a little blank.

"A' course we all know horses don't think," Swede said, beginning to sound like a lawyer himself, "but what would ya say if a human pulled off somethin' like that?"

"Something like, 'got rode the day she got sold'?" I asked a little derisively, impatient to get at the gist of what Swede was saying.

"The heart goes out of 'em!" Swede said and leaned over to spit in the dust as if that put a cap on his argument.

My translation read that while Swede was not actually accusing the Doll of taking a dive to queer the deal, he was convinced that the betrayal had somehow squelched the mare's fire. "How would she know about the deal anyway?" I asked him straight-faced.

"People talk," Swede said with a shrug. "Maybe she got it from the kids."

"Well, horses may think, but I never heard of one that could understand English." It was a simple statement on my part.

"Not in words," Swede stated impatiently. "Animals feel things like that: strange barn, strange handlers, maybe the kids got to see 'er one last time to say goodbye—when usually she'd be trippin' over 'em in 'er stall. It don't matter how she got wind of it; the point is, would she think anythin' of it?"

There was a point of logic in this that was difficult to argue with and Swede knew it.

"Why did they sell 'er off anyway?" I asked innocently.

Swede gave the rope a flip and his head a tired shake as if to say, "What's the use?"

"It was the Hungry Thirties," he said, coiling the rope. "A family livin' off the land like they were could hardly afford to keep an expensive buckin' horse like that when there was bills to pay."

"Must have been hard on the kids," I mused quietly.

"But not the mare," Swede said as Bender moved off, "cuz horses don't think."

* * *

Swede's exit left me with the distinct impression that there was still more to it than that; what that was, I decided not to ask. I knew Swede would have to talk about something, and if there really was something more to add to his argument in the Doll's story, it would come out.

But it didn't. Rail after rail, nail after nail...eventually I figured I'd been sweating for long enough and Swede had been sitting for long enough, that we might swap places.

"I'll do ya one better," Swede said enthusiastically. "Go on an' finish up what you're doin' there, an' I'll ride on down to the house an' get us a coupla cold beers."

Bender, as if he was in on it, had started wandering towards the house before Swede was finished talking about it. They came ambling back at the same speed, Swede tipping one beer to his lips and cradling another on the saddle horn. He looked like he'd never left the saddle, as if someone had passed him the beer from the front steps as he rode by, which they probably had.

I sat down in the shade to drink my beer. Swede rolled and lit a smoke without once letting go of the beer bottle.

"To the kids' old man," Swede said, right out of the blue, "she was a champion—the kind a' champion a man may be lucky enough to get to see once in his lifetime, let alone raise. To their mother, a fine woman, she was a mare, a fine mare! An' to the kids, a'course, she was just, the Doll…an', I imagine, in their own way they were all kinda proud of 'er as she went on down the road.

"As the reports filtered in from the big shows down south, it was a not half-bad consolation prize knowin' she was doin' well and bein' treated well—but this soured suddenly when they got word she had disappeared. The guy lost 'er down south a' Claresholm somewhere at some little punkin-roller rodeo—and keep in mind this is now a pretty famous and expensive chunk a' horseflesh—an' nobody sees 'er again."

Swede stepped down from the saddle, loosened Bender's cinch, then watched thoughtfully as the horse plodded contentedly over to the water trough.

"Until fall," Swede continued, "late in the fall, gettin' on towards winter…one a' the kids pitchin' hay outa the loft looks up to see a horse standin' at the gate at the end a' their driveway! An' them kids went tumblin' down that driveway an' wrapped themselves around them four legs just a-huggin' an' a-laughin' an' a-pushin' an' a-tuggin' the Doll home—now, I would like ya to tell me straight," Swede looked me in the eye, "how would that mare get the notion to come up with a trick like that—much less pull it off—without thinkin'?"

"Instinct?" I suggested rather lamely.

"Is that what ya call it?" Swede asked wryly.

"I don't know," I said. "I guess I never really thought much about it," which was true.

Swede gave a short whistle and Bender lifted his head to look back at him. Swede gave another, and, instinctively, as the horse began sauntering in our direction, I sensed that the beer break was over.

The Doc

It was late in October and the leaves, crimson and gold, clung perilously to the tree branches before the first blasts of winter. The late afternoon sun slanted through the ponderosa pines like blades of steel onto the spent grasses of the tawny meadows below. The girl, as still as the leaves, sat erect in the saddle absorbing what warmth the waning sun could afford. Only her eyes moved as methodically she counted, once more, the yearling horses grazing over the meadow before her.

"Twenty-six…five more to come, including…"

"A horse is a horse," as her father would always say. "Don't get attached to 'em."

But this was different, the girl told herself, and besides, she'd noticed that even her father didn't always practise what he preached.

It wasn't the money—although, for her, it had been a lot of money, in fact, all the money she'd ever managed to save. She'd

42

done well on her 4-H steers, babysitting for the Stattlers down the way—even most of her birthday money from Aunt May—and she'd plunked the whole thing down for stud fees…contrary to her father's repeated warnings and cautious pleas.

"It's your money," he'd said in the end, begrudgingly. It wasn't that she'd become overly attached, although she had to admit that right from the moment she'd laid eyes on the filly she'd been pleased. Neither had she found anything disappointing halter-breaking the filly after she'd been weaned. Even her father had to acknowledge the animal's good conformation, and the girl had found her to be just as quick to learn as she was quick on her feet.

The filly, the girl believed, had the gift of her breed—the Cutting Horse breed.

The girl remembered the first Cutting Horse she had ever seen. It was at a branding. Everyone had admired the horse's agility and cunning as it plied its trade in the hot dusty corral—but the girl had been mesmerized. The animal seemed to be able to move swifter than the cows and calves could think and with an economy and grace that left the girl imagining its unseen wings!

She had no complaints with Topper, the Quarterhorse gelding she was riding today. He was a good stock horse, honest and strong, and fast enough to have won her more than one gymkhana competition: First Prize for barrel racing.

They'd had lots of good horses—horses you could be proud of, like Black Jack, her father's rope horse that he was riding today—but that wasn't the point. The point was they weren't Cutting Horses. Mandy dreamed of someday sitting astride a real Cutting Horse as it performed its delicate ballet.

⁺ ✦ ⁺

A gangly-looking buckskin colt suddenly lifted his head to stare pop-eyed at the far end of the meadow. The herd followed suit, with a nervous nicker here and there, until all eyes and ears, including the girl's, were fixed in the same direction.

The girl tensed as she caught a small flicker of movement through the pines. The tension grew as she made out the small bunch of horses being driven like bad kids before her father and Black Jack.

Three…four—there were four for sure—there should be five. But as they broke into the meadow, they fanned out, racing to join the herd four abreast, and the charcoal filly was not one of them.

Black Jack cantered up to where the girl and Topper waited. Her father's eyes were fixed on the horses in the meadow and the girl gave him a moment or two before interrupting his gaze.

"Thirty…," she said calmly. He glanced at her sharply, the unspoken question etched darkly in his eyes.

"You sure?" he asked, looking back at the herd.

"Yes," she said.

"Damn," he muttered through clenched teeth and automatically looked to the sinking sun, noting the lengthening shadows of the pines. She knew he was calculating the time against the distance they still had to ride. They both knew he didn't have to ask which one was missing.

"I think I found out why they were so scattered," he said as a matter of interest. She waited. "I seen fresh cougar tracks down along the creek."

The girl's expression didn't change as she sat looking out over the frisky yearlings.

"Mandy," he said—her name was Madeline but nobody called her that except Aunt May—"for that horse to be separated off on 'er own like that; there'd have to be a good reason."

"Yes," she said, still looking out over the meadow.

"Well," he said with a burdened sigh, "let's get 'em home."

They bunched the herd and Mandy and Topper struck off in the lead with her dad and Black Jack pushing them from behind. Mandy loved herding horses, usually, especially these yearlings. It wasn't the kind of job you could get bored at. Everything happened at a brisk pace. But today neither the sound of the pounding hooves, nor the sight of the manes and tails flagging the trail behind her, could distract the morbid feeling that she was leaving something of herself behind.

* * *

It was a good two or three miles back to the ranch. There was a sharp right turn at the base of the river hills, and a dozen or so of the yearlings had missed it. She'd had to hold up in a hay field on the bottomland while her dad rounded up those that had strayed. The herd had become a little strung out fording the big creek, some stopping to drink, others racing on ahead—but all in all it was a good drive with nothing going seriously wrong.

Still, it was well after dark before they got in, once everything had been penned up and fed and the saddle horses squared away.

They got the usual scolding from Aunt May, as if they'd missed a hot supper on purpose—which the aunt had kept waiting for them anyway. Mandy wasn't very talkative and May thought she'd caught a chill and might be coming down with something. The woman started harping all over again on the folly of leaving a thirteen-year-old girl all alone in the middle of nowhere with ninety head of cattle to feed—"and God knows how many horses."

Yes, Mandy thought to herself, God did know exactly how many horses, and she made a mental note to bring it up with Him in her prayers before she went to bed that night.

"Are you two listening to me?" the aunt demanded suddenly.

"I'll be fine, Auntie May," Mandy said habitually.

"The Stattlers are just down the way—they'll be checking in on 'er, May," her father said from behind his newspaper.

May and her brother Fred, Mandy's father, were leaving the next morning and would be gone for three days. Fred had a trailer load of horses to haul down south and May was going to spend the time with their mother, Mandy's grandmother, who lived down that way. Aunt May had come to help out when Mandy's mother had died.

Mandy had been but a baby, and yet even after all that time, May still seemed to be there temporarily—just until things got back to "normal" again.

"And you promise me you'll stay off those horses while we're gone—I can't stand to think of you lying hurt somewhere and nobody around to know."

"I won't get hurt," Mandy said routinely. Her father was looking at her across the table. Neither of them had mentioned anything about the missing filly to May.

"She won't do anything stupid, will ya," said Fred, looking his daughter in the eye.

"Stupid? It's stupid to be leaving her here all alone in the first place—I just want a promise that she'll stay off those horses while we're gone."

"Now, May," said the brother, returning his attention to the paper, "you know this is the safest place in the world for a kid— if we were leaving her in the middle of the city you'd have something to worry about."

"Oh you're hopeless, the both of you," May said, gathering up the remains of the late supper.

* * *

They awoke the next morning to find that it had become colder and snowed a little in the night. It was a grey day. Mandy and Fred were out at first light to sort and load horses. Fred put out enough round bales, he figured, to last until Tuesday so that Mandy wouldn't have to start the tractor while he was gone.

"Just make sure they got water," he said. "We might be in for the big freeze." But he knew he really didn't have to remind her.

May had breakfast ready for them when they got in and insisted on putting the kitchen in order before she left.

Fred snatched up his town coat and overnight bag and headed out to warm up the truck, asking Mandy to bring out May's things. Mandy knew this meant he had something to say.

She picked up the old plaid suitcase with its tatters and stains and the matching vanity case and took them out to the truck where her dad stashed them behind the seat.

"I realize there's no point in telling you not to go looking for that horse," he said, gazing off in the direction of the lease, "cuz you probably would anyway. But I don't want you out there alone—you hear me?" He looked at her sternly.

"Yes," she said quietly.

"Take one of the Stattler kids with you," he continued, "and make sure you're back before dark, all right?"

"All right," she said, looking back towards the house where May had just bustled through the door, then stopped to do a last-minute inventory on the contents of her purse.

"And take a gun," said Fred quietly, and stepped up into the cab of the truck.

May came on like a whirlwind of last-minute hugs and kisses, smelling of the makeup she didn't usually wear, and again admonishing Mandy to stay off the horses.

"Let's go, May," her brother said patiently, with a wink and a smile at his daughter, and finally, they did.

Mandy went immediately down to the barn and threw her saddle on Black Jack. She tied on a lariat and halter, and a small sack of oats, and went back up to the house. There she stuffed some cookies and a couple of tea bags into a small pack sack. Out in the porch, she pushed her long legs (she was tall for her age) into her snowmobile pants and was buckling a pair of chaps on over these when the phone rang. She decided she wouldn't answer but gave in on the fourth ring. It was Trina Compton calling to invite her to a Halloween party the following Friday. Trina wanted to talk.

"…and you have to dress up," she said. "Everybody is."

Mandy assured her that she would be there, in costume, and broke off the conversation telling Trina some horses were out and she had to run.

Mandy did not bother to call the Stattlers. Those kids would only slow her down—but she did grab the 30.30 and a few shells on her way back through the porch.

She did not ride the same route they'd driven the yearlings back on the day before—that ground was covered. Rather, she rode out along the river—taking the low road, her dad called it—to the lease. She really didn't think the filly would have gone down over the banks, but, just in case.

Her plan was simple: ride the perimeters until she picked up a track. Of course she realized that was a lot of territory. She gave Black Jack a nudge in the ribs with her heels and he moved into travelling gait.

Halloween—Mandy had come to hate Halloween. Those years of climbing into the pickup with Aunt May and making the rounds to the neighbours. Aunt May, of course, had accepted the inevitable invitations for coffee at nearly every place—while Mandy sat munching on yet another chocolate bar or popcorn ball, dressed in some ridiculous costume…a costume—she'd told Trina she'd come to the party in costume! She couldn't think about all that just now. A party would be all right, to say nothing of a blessed relief from the Halloweens of the past—she'd declined to go out the last couple of years anyway. She'd phone Trina back tonight.

₊

They were now on the big flats adjacent to the lease. Mandy's eyes scanned the skiff of snow as it passed beneath Black Jack's feet. A moose, a coyote, several deer—but nothing that resembled a horse track.

Black Jack slipped and almost went down, climbing the steeply terraced land leading up to the lease. When they got to the top, Mandy headed west to the shack. A couple of times last summer she'd ridden out, caught up the filly and brought her down to the shack just to make sure she hadn't forgotten how to lead. She hadn't. Even catching her wasn't much of a problem with oats. Today, Mandy had a kind of a half-baked notion (which she didn't really believe) that the filly might have remembered the place and sought protection there when she couldn't find the rest of the horses on the lease.

Mandy poked her head in the door of the shack; the usual clutter and liberal sprinkling of mouse droppings. She dug a cookie out of her little pack and walked slowly down to the shed, letting Black Jack pluck at tufts of grass on the way.

The shed was a crude affair built of poles cut from the surrounding bush and covered in plywood sheets. It was just wide enough for two stalls and tall enough, on the high side, for a horse to stand with its head up. It leaked, here and there, in a good rain, but kept out the breeze. Mandy debated taking the five-gallon plastic pail as an oat pail, but decided it would be too noisy; the sack would do.

She mounted up and headed back east along the valley rim, stopping at lookouts along the way to scan the trees and meadows for…for ravens and magpies, she admitted to herself. A noisy cluster of scavengers like that would be something to investigate whether she wanted to or not—but she saw nothing.

She then rode north, crossing the path the herd had come home on the previous day. No lone track of a straggler greeted her hopeful eye.

At the north fence, they turned west again and headed into the pines. The sky was a shroud of grey. She couldn't tell where the sun was, but knew the day was passing. She had never actually been to the farthest northwest corner of the lease. It was mostly muskeg swamp and didn't make for good riding. Of course, today, it would be mostly frozen. She debated turning south back towards the shack or carrying on through the swamps to the end of the fence line. She decided to stick to her plan. Once they started riding willy-nilly all over the place they'd soon be riding over their own tracks, learning nothing.

It seemed to grow darker riding through the swamps under an alder canopy. "Good moose pasture," her father would say.

She was just starting to expect the western fence line when crossing a boggy little creek she noticed a track that stopped her cold. She got down off her horse to take a closer look. There in the snow were the unmistakable pug-marks of a cougar—a big cougar, it seemed to Mandy, and the hair began to rise on the back of her neck sending a shiver down her spine. The cougar was heading south back across the lease.

"Headed back south of the river," Mandy guessed, or hoped. Up until now, she'd believed the animal had been just sort of "passing through" and maybe it'd taken a run at the herd of yearlings, scattering them like her father had said, or maybe it hadn't.

Spring before last, a cougar had taken a newborn colt. Her dad had tracked it back to the river where he'd decided to let it pass. A female, he'd figured, with a den somewhere up on the other side. "The price of doing business out here," he'd said. "We don't pay nothing for the rain."

Of course, if "the price" had gone up she knew her dad would have been waiting with his .308—but they hadn't seen any further sign of the cougars that spring.

A new idea occurred to the girl. If this cougar had made a kill it could just be returning to it for its supper. All Mandy would have to do to find out was follow this track. She didn't think the cougar would attack her on Black Jack—it would probably just run for its life—she did have the old 30.30…but it seemed so dark; what time was it anyway? She would probably just be getting off the bus if it was a school day.

For the first time, she wished she'd brought somebody along. To ride in on an animal like that on a kill, she might surprise it, forcing it to strike—and if it had made a kill, she really didn't want to find it anyway.

She decided to ride on and a short distance later came to the western fence line. She turned south and urged Black Jack to pick up his faltering gait. She thought of the cookies, and oats for the horse, but decided they had to make time. The land was opening up a bit. There was a smattering of giant pines among the willow crowns and poplar trees.

For the second time that day the sight of a track stopped her. But this time, it was human. Something about finding a human footprint out here in the middle of nowhere…

The track came over the barbed wire and headed east onto their lease. Mandy thought she knew who it was, but the thought didn't give her complete relief.

Stanley Spratt was his name—the Stattler kids called him Stanley Bat, and it wasn't hard to imagine why. The man had a small pinched face and the whitest skin Mandy had ever seen. Stanley wore an oversized pair of sunglasses, the kind you could see yourself in, which were much too large for his face. People said that he only went out at night or on especially dark days—like this one, Mandy thought—and that was why his skin was so white. But her dad said there was something wrong with his eyes that made them sensitive to bright light. Stanley worked the trapline west of the lease and sometimes stopped by their place. Mandy shuddered at the thought of arriving home to find Stanley Bat waiting for her. But the man was very shy and though he and her father were friends, in an odd sort of way, she knew that if no one else was around, he wouldn't stay. The Stattler kids were afraid of him.

As Mandy rode on, she began to wish that she'd never left the ranch. What good was she doing out here anyway? Maybe she just needed a cookie, she thought, and a nice hot cup of tea. Black Jack suddenly drew up short, ears erect, staring into the dark of the pines. Mandy nudged him in the ribs and slacked the reins, but he refused to budge. Black Jack was too well trained to spook at an oddball stump or the falling leaves. Mandy began to reach for the 30.30 but froze as her eyes detected movement at close range. Slowly the man emerged from behind the trunk of a large pine tree not twenty yards away.

"Hello," said Stanley Spratt.

"Hello," said Mandy, her voice sounding hollow, as if coming from far away.

"Sorry I scared you," said Stanley, and bowed his head slightly.

"You didn't scare me, you scared my horse," Mandy answered, trying to sound like it.

"You got a horse out," Stanley said apologetically.

"What?" Mandy said, a thrill of hope shooting straight up from her half-frozen toes.

"Some hunters came through on quads the other day—left a gate down. I just found it today." Stanley seemed to be looking at the ground, but it was hard to tell what his eyes were doing behind those ridiculous shades.

"What horse?" Mandy almost shouted.

"I just seen its track going out through the gate—I left it open in case it tried to come back through, but I figured I should come an' check if you got any more stock in here, 'n case it got out too."

"We don't have any," Mandy said impatiently. "Where's that horse now?"

"Probably not far," Stanley said with a shrug, "you'll cross its track up there at the gate."

"Thanks," said Mandy, and jammed her heels into Black Jack's sides. "Thanks a lot," she shouted, as they galloped past the man standing with his head down next to the big pine.

In minutes, she was at the open gate and there, sure enough, were the tracks of a single horse leading out through the middle of it. But as Mandy scrutinized the hoof prints more closely, her excitement was dampened considerably. There was something wrong. She dismounted and walked for a ways, studying the marks in the snow to discern their meaning. It seemed to her that the yearling was more or less dragging its right hind leg. In fact, it was getting too dark to see, but Mandy doubted whether the horse was really stepping down on that leg at all. Darkness! A wave of panic swept over the girl, and she quickly swung up into the saddle and took off as fast as she could go without losing sight of the tracks.

The tracks seemed to be following the trail along the rim of the river valley that Mandy knew ultimately led to Stanley Spratt's. The trapper's cabin was on a high point of land overlooking the river valley. Was that where the filly was heading? Then suddenly the tracks disappeared. Mandy jumped down to take a closer look. It was getting darker by the minute. Nothing! She began back-tracking, leading Black Jack, straining to see where the young mare's hoof mark had ended. Near panic, she began walking faster, almost running, when Black Jack started to lag. She turned to give him a jerk on the reins and saw that his head was up and he was looking off into a swampy meadow beside the trail. The big horse gave a low nicker that, before the girl could even think, was answered by a high-pitched whinny!

Mandy almost shouted for joy! She peered through the gathering dark, unable to make out anything against the banks of trees surrounding the meadow.

"Whoa, girl," she said softly. "Whoa now." She stepped over beside Black Jack and, placing her gloves on the seat of the saddle, felt out the frozen leather ties that held the oat sack. Black Jack nickered again, this time at the rustling of the oats, and again the filly answered. Mandy still couldn't see anything, but marked the direction of the sound and the distance—close, very close!

Finally, she freed the oat sack and the halter and stepped off the trail into the meadow. She moved slowly on the uncertain footing, staring into the dark for the young charcoal mare.

"Whoa, girl," she repeated softly. She'd gone as far as she dared without further bearings. Black Jack began crowding her in search of the oats. She reached up and gave him a light slap on the nose. He hadn't seen it coming and gave a start that in turn set off a rustling in the grass of the meadow close at hand.

Shadows upon shadows, but one of them was moving not twenty feet away. "Whoa, girl, whoa," Mandy said, shaking the oat sack lightly and beginning to circle in front of the yearling, which stopped. Seconds later, she was nuzzling oats from the girl's hand and a minute after that Mandy had slipped the halter over her head. She had her!

The shack wasn't far back up the trail, but it was slow going. The yearling limped badly, but in the dark, Mandy still couldn't tell whether she was putting any weight on that leg. When they finally reached the shack the girl tied the horses outside the shed. She opened the door and, feeling her way, divided the oats between the two oat boxes in the crude mangers at the head of each stall. She then let in Black Jack, stripped off the saddle and bridle and tied him into the far stall. The filly offered no resistance to being led into the shed, but seemed eager to catch up with her share of the oats, which Mandy took as a good sign.

Snatching her little pack sack off the saddle, Mandy headed up to the shack. She fumbled through the drawers and cupboards until she finally found and lit a candle. She then lit a fire in the airtight heater. It was only when the fire began to give off the first heat that Mandy realized how cold she was, and hungry, and thirsty. She'd watered Black Jack at the spring out back of the shack; the young mare didn't drink.

The girl was shivering violently when she got back with the water and didn't stop until she'd downed her first cup of tea and fourth cookie. She flipped the mattress on the bottom bunk to avoid the mouse droppings and unravelled the snare wire that suspended the bundle of blankets from a beam above her head.

Her body was aching to sleep, but her mind would not rest until she'd made one more trip down to the shed. Wire cut, bowed tendon, a frozen stick jammed up in the frog? It could be any of these things—it could be none of them. Maybe she'd just taken a good kick from one of the other horses and was being a big baby about it. Mandy had to have a look.

She held the candle before her, cupping her free hand around the flame to keep it from going out. The light and shadows ran before her, leaping at the trees and into the starless sky above. Somehow the light spooked her where the dark hadn't.

She opened the door of the shed and stepped in, holding the candle aloft…and froze.

The velvety charcoal coat was slashed by three parallel claw marks that grew into one large gaping gash of proud flesh and dried blood over the haunch. The swelling, Mandy knew, meant that infection was starting to set in. Halfway down the leg was a second cut, spiralling from the front inside towards the rear tendons. Mandy couldn't tell if a tendon had been cut—there was swelling there too—the yearling held the leg up, resting the toe of the hoof, pointed downward, on the floor of the shed.

Mandy felt sick. She backed out of the shed and turned towards the shack. The candle flickered and died, but the girl scarcely noticed. At the shack, she dropped the candle onto the table and felt her way to her bunk.

"Why?" Why, out of all those scrub ponies and broomtails…

She felt betrayed. She felt like crying—but crying wasn't what you did when a horse got hurt. Maybe she was crying, what of it?!

Sleep finally claimed her. Crying…a baby? Crying? Something had woken her up.

Her eyes were open wide—not that it made any difference; it was obviously still night…it cried again! "Oh God," the girl said aloud. "The cougar!" Her dad said they could make a sound like that—she flew to the door to check the bolt; it was locked!

The sound came again, sounding more like a snarl.

The horses! Had she latched the door shut when she left the shed?

The rifle! Where was the rifle? It was in its scabbard, tied to the saddle, which was out in the shed with the horses!

Terror swept over the girl and with it a panicky wave of impulses. Should she make a run for the shed—light the candle—light the fire—light a torch? The cougar snarled again, sounding closer—or was it? How close was closer?

It was there, in the dark, sniffing out the prey that had somehow escaped it earlier—prey that was now tied up waiting for him, behind a door that wasn't even latched! Or was it? Why couldn't she remember? The girl sank, slowly, to the floor against the door of the shack.

A rifle shot went off, sounding like the whole world had exploded, and Mandy screamed! For a moment she just crouched there against the door, in shock.

Stanley, Stanley Bat; it had to be! Mandy leapt to her feet, running her hands over the table top until she found the candle and a wooden match. She lit the candle and took it with her to the door that she unbolted and opened.

"Stanley?" she called into the dark, startled by the sound of her own voice. "Stanley Spratt!"

"Hello," said a voice close at hand, and Mandy started again. She raised the candle and peered into the dark. The man was hard to find in his dark coat and fur hat, but his face shone like a pearl. It was the first time Mandy had seen him without the sunglasses.

"Did you get the cougar?" Mandy asked hopefully.

"Too dark," said Stanley. "But I gave 'im a good scare. He won't be back."

"What are you doing out here?" Mandy was still somewhat in shock.

"Well, I'm, we're neighbours," Stanley said. "I live just down the valley rim here."

"I know that," Mandy said impatiently, "I mean what were you doing out here, tonight, now?"

"Well," Stanley looked off into the dark, "When I seen that cougar's tracks today, I figured he might be lookin' for the same horse you were. I guess he was too."

"Yes," said Mandy, gratitude welling up in her all over again. "Can I get you a cup of tea?"

"No," said Stanley. "I better be getting home."

"Thank you, Mr. Spratt." It was Mandy's turn to look away. "Thanks a lot."

"Good night," said Stanley Bat, and turned away, disappearing into the night.

"Good night," Mandy called after him, and closed the door. She kindled the fire in the airtight, put on the tea and sat down to think. The young mare's needs, she knew, went well beyond her expertise—beyond her father's even—and that infection wouldn't wait until Tuesday in any case.

There'd have to be some stitching done, and somebody would have to look at those tendons to judge whether any of the rest of it was even worthwhile. Veterinarians in general were out of the question. Her father didn't believe in them. "Just throwin' good money after bad even talkin' to them," she'd often heard him say. "They'll think nothin' ah chargin' ya twice what a calf is worth to save it, and if they happen to kill the cow in the process, that's yer problem!"

But with "the Doc" he made an exception. "He'll take one look and tell ya straight out where you stand—and ya don't have to mortgage the ranch just to talk to 'im, either!" Just last spring, her father had called on the Doc for a bull with a split toe.

But, would he even come out to the lease? As far as she knew, most veterinarians asked that you bring the animal in—and how would she pay him? She'd have to work on that.

* ⋆ *

The sky was lighting up. She led Black Jack out, saddled him and then let him graze behind her as she picked grass for the filly. She watered her out of the pail, then making sure she was locked in securely, mounted Black Jack and rode hard for the ranch.

Once there she went directly to the house and dug out her father's little black book. She couldn't remember the Doc's last name, but knowing her dad looked under "D" for Doc. There it was: "Doc Somerville" with two phone numbers written beside it. She dialled the first number and waited. It rang and rang, but no one answered. It was Sunday. The second number must be his home—Mandy almost lost her nerve, then quickly dialled. On the third ring a man answered.

"Is Doc Somerville there?" Mandy asked.

"You're talking to him."

"Oh, hello," said the girl. "This is Mandy McCullough—Fred McCullough's daughter, out in Silver Valley?"

"Yeah, I know Fred," said the Doc.

"A cougar took a swipe at one of our horses and cut her up a bit, and we need you to take a look at her," Mandy said. "If you could, I mean," she added. "Doc?"

"Yeah," said the Doc. "I was just thinking that would mean I'd have to miss church, again."

"Oh," Mandy said.

"But that's all right," said Somerville. "I'll go twice next Sunday. Should be out there in about an hour."

"Thank you," Mandy said calmly, and hung up the phone. He was coming.

She raced out of the house, led Black Jack down to the barn and fed him, royally. She then went back to the house and did the same for herself—she was famished. Next, she caught up Topper, checking on the way to make sure the cows had water;

they did. She saddled Topper, then dug the old toboggan out of the shed and lashed on a bale of hay and one of straw with binder twine.

By the time the Doc's battered white sports sedan turned into the driveway, she was waiting at the house with the toboggan and the two horses saddled and ready.

"Hello there," said the Doc, pushing open the door. "I take it you're Mandy?"

"Yes," she said.

The Doc didn't get out of the car, but began rummaging through a black leather bag he'd pulled over onto his lap. He was dressed in a white western shirt with a string tie, polished cowboy boots and dress slacks.

"How's your dad?" asked Doc, still pawing through the bag.

"Oh, he's fine," Mandy said. "We'd really like to thank you for coming out on a Sunday."

"Oh, that's nuthin'," said the Doc, opening up the glove compartment and commencing to paw through that.

"Normally my dad wouldn't be spending money on a yearling—mare to boot—but she's a purebred Cutting Horse."

The Doc cocked his head and looked at her, causing his jowls to sag to one side.

"Yeah?" he said. "How much money do you figure he's ready to spend, abnormally speaking?"

"Oh, she's not that bad really, Doc. When you see her you'll see what I mean—considering it was a cougar and everything."

"Where'd you say Fred was again?" the Doc asked, returning his attention to the glove compartment. He withdrew a handful of paraphernalia and stuffed it into the black bag.

"He's just down south with the horses," Mandy answered.

"Down south...," the Doc pondered. "How far down south?"

"High River," she said, looking at the toe of her boot.

"Ahhh," said Doc as if that explained everything. "About six hundred miles south, then."

"Yes," Mandy said.

"Well," said Doc, snapping the black bag shut. "Let's have a look at the patient!"

"Well," Mandy said haltingly, "she's down on the lease."

"What?" said the vet.

"The filly is in the shed down on our grazing lease."

"Ah, so she's down south too!" said Doc.

"West," Mandy said quietly.

"And, I suppose, that's what those two saddle horses are for?" asked the veterinarian. "Maybe I should have gone to church," he mumbled, climbing out of the car. He reached into the back seat and pulled out a beaded moosehide jacket and bent Stetson. "And just how far west is the lease?" he asked, pulling on the jacket.

"Oh, it's just over the creek and up the hill, and a little ways past that," Mandy said excitedly.

The Doc reached back into the car and took what looked, to Mandy, to be a bottle of liquor from the console. "Antifreeze," the man said, stuffing the bottle into the leather bag. "Lead on."

Mandy grew talkative on the way to the lease. She recounted her search for the filly and the cat-and-mouse game the cougar had played. The Doc seemed mildly attentive as he rode along on Topper. Mandy set a good travelling pace on Black Jack, who took no notice of the lariat tied to the saddle horn and the toboggan behind.

The Doc seemed not to notice the cold. Mandy noted his gloveless hands, pot belly protruding from the open moosehide and the red glow of his nose and cheeks. She noted as well that he did make liberal and frequent reference to his supply of "antifreeze."

Mandy turned the subject to Cutting Horses, updating the Doc, completely, on the wonders of the breed—and suddenly they were there.

Mandy jumped down and tied the saddle horses to nearby trees, then anxiously threw open the door of the shed. The filly looked back at them and gave a soft neigh.

"Well, Doc," said Mandy, "what do you think?"

"Well," said the Doc, "I think we should get 'er out here in the light. You can spread that straw bale for her over there, and tie her up to that tree."

Mandy moved quickly. By the time she had the filly standing in straw, the Doc had removed his jacket, which he hung on a branch of the tree, and rolled up his shirt sleeves. He'd taken a small vial and syringe from the bag and was filling one from the other.

"What are you going to do?" asked Mandy.

"We're just going to put 'er to sleep for a bit," said the Doc, intent on his work.

"Oh," said Mandy, her face clouding over. "Do we have to? I've heard it's dangerous, to their hearts or something?"

"Yeah?" said the Doc. "Well, I've heard it's dangerous to go cuttin' into a wound on a horse's back leg if the horse is standing there wide awake looking at ya!" He moved into position at the filly's head and began stroking her softly. "We could tie up the leg," he said quietly, "but she'd probably get thrashin' and do herself more harm before we could do 'er any good."

"Can we, Doc?" Mandy asked in a small voice.

"Can we what?" the Doc asked absent-mindedly.

"Do her any good?" said Mandy.

"Course we can," he answered, plunging in the needle and following the horse as she pulled back. "Get ready to loosen off on her head, there!" the vet said, withdrawing the needle.

A few minutes later the young mare was asleep on the straw.

"We're gonna need some warm water," said the Doc. He held his hands, and a cruel-looking knife, out over the horse's wounds while dousing them in a foul-smelling antiseptic he'd taken from his bag.

Mandy hurried to the shack where she started a fire, then on to the spring. The Doc was kneeling over the filly's hindquarters, blood up to his elbows, by the time Mandy returned with the bucket of warm water.

The Doc groaned as he straightened up. He dumped a liberal dosage of antiseptic into the water, then splashed a good quantity of the mixture over his carvings. He then told Mandy to hold out her hands, which he also baptized, and sending her around to the yearling's other side, began ordering her to pull on "this" and hold on to "that" while he commenced stitching.

"Just going to tack her together here and there," he explained. "We'll leave it open so it can drain—you'll have to watch it and keep it clean."

By the time the Doc straightened up, with another groan, Mandy was sweating.

"There," he said, and plunged his hands into what water and disinfectant remained. He also rinsed his knife.

The mare was starting to stir by the time he pulled out the needle again. "I'll leave you some of this," he said, jabbing the syringe into a muscle. She'll need a shot a day for about a week."

They were done. "She'll be tryin' to get up in a minute or two," said the Doc, stuffing the syringe into the black bag. "Give 'er some water and a little hay, and tie her back up to that tree." He then retrieved his jacket and made for the shack while rolling down his shirt sleeves.

When Mandy came in, he was warming his feet against the airtight and warming the rest of his anatomy with a coffee cup full of his antifreeze.

"She's up," said the girl.

"Good," said the vet with a nod.

Mandy set a pot of water on for tea and, sitting down opposite the Doc, asked cautiously, "Do you think she's going to be all right?"

"Well," said the Doc, tipping his chair back comfortably, "there's never any guarantees—but I'd say she'll be just fine." It seemed it was the Doc's turn to grow talkative. "You know, from the look of those paw prints," he said, "I'd be willing to bet that cougar took a pretty good kick in the teeth!" He then went on to explain, using his arms to illustrate, what he surmised had been the cougar's reach and where that would have placed it in relation to the yearling's hind feet. "She was lucky," he said. "It would have been a different story if he'd been successful in clipping a hamstring." The Doc declined the tea but did add some hot water to his antifreeze.

Mandy was pleased, but there was one more ominous item of business that she decided she might as well face. "How much do we owe you, Doc?" she asked, trying to sound like it was a mere point of curiosity.

"Oh, that," said the Doc. "Well, it was no big chore, really…I'll tell you what," he said as if struck by a sudden inspiration, "I haven't got my moose yet this year. If I could come out and camp for a few days in this place, I might just rectify that situation."

"Sure!" said Mandy. "Anytime."

"Well, you tell your old man we'll call it even, if he supplies the antifreeze."

"He'll be back Tuesday," Mandy said eagerly.

"No rush," said the Doc. "I should check on that filly in a week or so anyways."

They emerged from the shack to find the young mare steady on her feet and sampling the hay. The Doc declared they could try leading her home—which they did, slowly but surely, arriving well before dark. Mandy saw the Doc off, then put the filly to bed in a box stall stuffed with fresh straw and hay.

She then went in and fixed herself some of her own favourite things to eat. She knew she was tired, perhaps more tired than she'd ever been, but somehow she didn't feel like sleep.

She phoned Trina Compton. They chatted aimlessly, touching on this and that, eventually striking on the subject of Trina's party.

"What are you wearing?" Trina asked pointedly.

"I'm coming as Stanley Bat," said Mandy.

Suburban
Blue

*L*ydia Flicker's pride in their new Cape Cod-style bungalow with its immaculate plastic siding and plastic spindles on its token veranda was only equalled by her pride in its immaculate landscaping. So when she chanced to cast an admiring glance through the bulging bay window to behold a monstrous beast indiscriminately helping itself to a casual mouthful of their immaculate lawn, her first reaction was an involuntary scream.

The horse, a mottled blue roan-cum-Appaloosa, jerked its head up at the sound to gaze about in search of its source. Not thinking to look in the window it lost interest and heaving a contented sigh resumed munching the close-cropped carpet at its feet.

Lydia, recoiling in shock at the horrific spectacle, seemed momentarily overcome. Clearly she had never imagined a cataclysm of such catastrophic proportions. Valiantly she had battled the redoubtable dandelion—spraying, uprooting and spraying again until she could say with proud confidence that she had banned the yellow menace from her yard. Fairy rings, the moulds of spring and winterkill she had taken on and vanquished in their turn; but now this?

It wasn't until the horrid beast, ambling over to browse through the tastefully appointed flowerbed, came up with a mouthful of nasturtiums that Lydia erupted into action.

Bursting through the front door onto the veranda while emitting the plaintive cry of "Shooo!" she succeeded only in startling the animal into one involuntary leap forward, which landed it among the flowers it had been sampling.

From there it gazed back at the woman in wide-eyed surprise, one orange blossom still protruding from the corner of its mouth.

"Shoo," Lydia repeated with a perfunctory wave of her hand.

A stand-off ensued—Lydia having exhausted her vocabulary of horse commands; the horse apparently unable to interpret the one she offered. The stand-off ended with Lydia retreating into the safety of her house where she paced in front of the bay window. The blue roan, having shaken off the interruption with a snort, resumed its inspection of the flowers.

That most unwelcome of thoughts—"What will the neighbours think?"—crept into the woman's mind, tempting her to despair as she looked down the long curving row of similar houses and similar lawns that enclosed her street.

At almost the same instant the incongruity of the thing struck her along with the idea that a horse definitely constituted an illegal hazard to horticulture in the suburbs and as such it should be summarily dealt with by the authorities. But what authorities? Her husband would know.

Bill Flicker was a man of some importance in the bank that occupied a stall in the neighbourhood strip mall. At the tender age of thirty-two he had already attained the title, and the awesome responsibilities that came with it, of "Loans Manager."

In fact, at that very moment he was engaged in the ominous task of refusing a loan to an eager young couple attempting to purchase their first home—challenging work requiring a high degree of concentration and presence of mind.

When his desk phone rang he did not answer but left that to someone in the outer office who would realize that he was in a meeting. It rang again only moments later, disturbing Flicker's concentration and causing him to glance impatiently through the glass cubicle that set him apart from the rest. Scanning the ordinary personnel of the outer office, his eyes met Thelma's. She held the receiver of her phone aloft and looked back at Flicker as the phone on his desk continued to proclaim her insistence that the call was for him.

Bill frowned at her pointedly, and marshalling his powers of concentration, resumed his informative, if disappointing, discourse with the young couple. The ringing ceased. Bill noted that Thelma had spoken to the caller but was further distracted when she rose laboriously from her swivel chair and began making her way directly to his door. She opened the door without knocking and her tone betrayed a slight impatience of her own as she informed him that it was his wife on line one. The woman closed the door and turned her back on him before he could object, forcing him to apologize to the undeserving couple before him for the interruption.

His greeting took the form of a curt announcement to the effect that he was in a meeting and would have to call her back. But in the next instant he seemed confused, if not stunned, by her rejoinder. The important array of papers before him disappeared from his view, as did the man and woman across the desk, while his brain grappled with Lydia's cryptic announcement.

"There's a what, eating our what?" Lydia's clarification, while it did not explain the situation to Bill's complete satisfaction, did impart something of the urgent nature of the problem. "Have you tried chasing it away?" he asked, attempting to regain something of the official bearing that went with his office.

"It won't go," Lydia explained.

The couple opposite him exchanged questioning glances, bringing Bill back to the task that lay before him.

"I'll have to call you back," he repeated firmly, and then, poised to hang up, added, "Call the police."

Back in the bay window Lydia was beside herself. The blue roan, having ambled lazily through the flowerbed, had now made its way into the alcove adjacent to the carport. There it had begun maliciously munching the exotic grasses Lydia and Bill had painstakingly coaxed into existence in strategic locations in the rock garden.

Outraged at what she perceived to be the criminal indifference of her mate, Lydia frantically flipped through the pages of the phone directory. Having located and dialled the number for the R.C.M.P., and upon hearing it answered by an official-sounding female voice, Lydia dutifully, if not a bit rapidly, recited her full name and address, "…and there is a horse in my rock garden!" Speaking the thing out loud brought home the injustice of the vile outrage, bringing Lydia to the brink of tears.

Now, it is one of the modern idiosyncrasies of the small northern city that the Flickers called home that when a resident dials what they believe to be their local constabulary the call is actually received by a dispatcher in the city of Edmonton some three hundred miles to the south. The Royal Canadian Mounted Policewoman, mounted, presumably, on a desk chair in some downtown office, could therefore be forgiven for not immediately grasping the full import of the situation.

"Could you repeat that please," the policewoman said after a slight delay.

"I said," Lydia responded, "I have a horse in my garden!"

"I'm sorry," said the policewoman after a slightly longer pause. "Are you asking if it's legal to keep a horse in your yard?"

"Legal?" Lydia erupted. "Of course it's not legal! And I want it removed immediately!"

"I see," said the woman somewhat unconvincingly. "And whose horse would this be?"

"How should I know whose horse it is," Lydia almost shouted into the mouthpiece. "The point is that I'm demanding you get someone over here to take it away!"

"May I have your phone number please?"

To Lydia's ear the woman sounded as if she was filling out forms or something.

"My phone number? What good is that going to do? Do you understand that I have a horse outside my window as we speak?"

"Yes, I understand that, but I still require you to give me your phone number."

Lydia gave it to her. The policewoman informed Lydia that she would be contacted, and hung up.

Lydia wanted to cry. In fact, she would have just sat right down and had a good cry but for the growing outrage she felt at the pure injustice of the crime in progress.

The phone rang. Lydia nearly leapt down the caller's throat, ready to demand action. However, it was not the policewoman but Bill. He then made the mistake of telling Lydia to calm down.

"Calm down!?" Lydia roared. "Do you understand that this horse is at this very moment…" There was a long pause during which time a bolt of fear shot through Bill Flicker.

"Lydia?!" It was as if the line had been cut.

"…gone," said Lydia.

"What?" Bill's voice finally betrayed the sense of urgency his wife thought had been missing earlier.

"The horse is gone," Lydia said, somewhat dazed by the mystery of it all.

"Gone where?" Bill demanded, resuming some of the air of importance that went with his position at the bank.

"How should I know? Why should I care? The point is, it's—"

She was cut short by a frantic scream coming from the direction of her back door.

She flew to the door and opened it, without even imagining the source and cause of the scream, to find her neighbour Hazel Prestige flattened against it. The woman, while pursuing her habitual course to Lydia's door, had apparently come very close to rear-ending the infamous blue roan, which stared back at her from the lawn next to the herb garden.

"Lydia! What's going on?" Bill's voice sounded distant and mousy through the telephone receiver that Lydia still clutched in her hand as she admitted Hazel to the safety of the kitchen.

"What…?" the visibly shaken Hazel sought explanation.

"It's a horse," Lydia said matter-of-factly, and clapped the phone to her ear. "He's now going for the herb garden, Bill!"

"I'll be there as soon as I can," Bill said, rising from his desk.

"As soon as you can?" Lydia said in a tone that clearly indicated that she was not to be trifled with.

"Now," Bill explained. "I'm leaving now."

* ⋆ *

Meanwhile, Stump Torgeson was out at the stockyards adjoining the auction mart on the north end of town miserably prowling the pens and corrals in search of the "damned blue roan with the wall-eye." He got the name "Stump" roping a one-ton Red Angus bull, which is very similar to roping a passing one-ton truck. His horse gave a jump, slacking the dally 'round the saddle horn, and Torgeson had pulled back a stump where his right thumb had been. Stump was one of those guys who, if you didn't really know him, you might think had the permanent disposition of a badger with heartburn. Once you got to know him, you'd realize it was more like a scalded badger with heartburn and you could get heartburn yourself just listening to him—which most of the crew around the auction mart tried to avoid as much as possible. He'd interrogated everybody in the place in his search for the horse. He was accusing them of leaving gates open until finally discovering the tracks that clearly indicated that the horse had jumped the back fence and ambled on down the railroad tracks in the direction of town.

"Dirty Dyin' Dora," Stump had exclaimed, and issuing a long series of oaths and complaints had climbed into the old pickup with the stock racks on the back and headed into town.

* ⋆ *

The police had phoned back referring Lydia to the city's Animal Control Office, which Lydia had then phoned with some enthusiasm. However, in the ensuing discussion with Animal Control Officer Delilah Sempovitch, Lydia had somehow discovered the woman's impressive title to be nothing more than a euphemism for dogcatcher, whereupon Lydia had vented her frustrations upon the poor woman, hung up on her and called the police back. Lydia also hung up on the R.C.M.P. who continued to guarantee nothing.

"Can I use the phone for a second?" asked Hazel, who now seemed to be enjoying the spectacle of the thing.

"Hello Irene? It's Hazel. I'm over at the Flickers'. You have got to come over and see what they've got in their yard."

"Hazel!" Lydia shouted, horrified.

"Well, I just thought she'd…."

Lydia was beginning to look dangerous when the appearance of Bill in the driveway sent her bolting through the front door.

"Phone the police, you said!"

"Now, Lydia, calm down," cringed Bill. "I'm sure it's not all that serious that we can't—"

"Serious?" Lydia clamped onto her husband's hand and commenced dragging him through the carport into the back yard, where both were silenced by what they saw.

The horse, having wandered into the patch that represented the very trendy collection of herbs and other little exotics, had just hoisted its tail and was in the process of defecating on the mint and parsley.

* ⋆ *

Stump had been prowling the neighbourhood for some time when he came across the scene that had evolved in front of the Flickers' residence. He recognized it immediately.

"Dirty Dyin' Dora," he muttered as the old pickup coasted to a stop between the R.C.M.P. cruiser, a bylaw enforcement mini-van and sundry other neighbours and onlookers. No one even took notice as he snatched a halter and shank off the seat beside him and strode through the crowd.

The dogcatcher seemed to be in an argument with the owners, who were obviously furious, and the R.C.M.P. constable was engaged in keeping curious onlookers back from the danger area represented by the roan. Stump did not stop to introduce himself but breezed past everyone while glaring at the horse.

"Damn you for a wall-eyed broomtail fence-jumpin' cayuse," he muttered to himself as he walked up to the animal, clamped the halter on its head and with one vicious jerk on the shank began leading it out of the yard.

The gaggle of onlookers parted like the Red Sea as horse and man ambled through the carport and on down the driveway.

At the truck, Stump threw open the gate to the stock racks, threw the halter over the animal's neck, and giving it a kick in the hindquarters growled, "Git up there."

The roan, who seemed to have had previous experience with this man, complied immediately. Stump slammed the gate shut, climbed into the cab and threw 'er in gear before anyone in attendance at the crisis could collect themselves. They gazed dumbfounded at the blue roan disappearing down the block in the cloud of blue smoke that trailed behind the old truck.

"Dirty Dyin' Dora," Stump muttered to himself as he glanced into the side mirror to see if they were being followed—they weren't.

The Lost
Trail

*D*read. Dread of the packhorse that had never been packed. Dread of the rivers they would have to swim, which neither Luke nor James had ever seen. Dread of the grizzly that had dogged their tracks. And now, dread at the prospect of telling Jonas they had failed.

Failed? Or had they been beaten? What was the difference? To Jonas it would mean that he was hauling the outfit back from the starting line instead of the finish line and there didn't seem to be an excusable way of phrasing an explanation.

The Edson Trail had been the last great wagon trail in the history of the West—two hundred and fifty miles of muskeg, foothills, rivers and streams stretching from Edson (the railhead in 1911) to Sturgeon Lake due north and ending fifty or sixty miles west of there at the present site of the city of Grande Prairie.

From about 1911 to 1916, when the railroad penetrated the Peace Country, covered wagons, ox carts, the mail stage, pack

71

trains and even hikers with pack dogs trailing behind, had streamed over the trail chasing tales of "free land" in a sod-busters' paradise.

Jonas had driven one of those wagons as a boy of fourteen. That was the main reason why, for a nominal fee, he had agreed to haul the horses and assist the boys in finding a "jumping-off" place. A halfway house or some old bridge pilings would authenticate a site and help indicate the whereabouts of "the Trail" or its last remains.

The trail had, of course, been lost. At least, its exact location through the endless muskegs and dense lowlands between Edson and Sturgeon Lake had been thankfully abandoned and never brought to mind after the arrival of the train. Since then, most of that territory had remained a gloriously trackless waste. It was said that pianos, off-loaded into swamps in 1915, now protruded with incongruity from muskeg hummocks in tamarack shade; farm implements remained imbedded in the trunks of eighty-foot trees; and chests of settlers' effects (china, tools and valuables) were left cached and never claimed.

* ⋆ *

Tales like these had sparked the imaginations of Luke and James (an artist and a writer, respectively). What they lacked in wrangler know-how, they felt they could make up with enthusiasm and a dream—especially Luke.

Being an artist, and therefore favouring the visual side of things, Luke had shown up on departure day wearing a buckskin shirt glazed with dirt, leggings to match, lace-up riding boots, a ten-gallon (at least) hat and, underneath it all, red woollen long johns (despite the near ninety-degree heat).

To top it all off, from behind the seat of his car, he produced a sawed-off 4.10 shotgun in a homemade bearskin holster, which he proudly strapped to his waist!

More dread. When queried as to the status of the shotgun he confessed that it was in fact loaded at all times.

"Bird shot in one barrel; slug in the other—pick up a little meat along the way," was what he had said, and had then refused to discuss it further.

Though Jonas was now well into his eighties, he still not only rode but broke horses, and not with any newborn degree of science or technique but in the legendary and old-fashioned way: from the "hurricane deck" (what he called the saddle).

So, while it was true that the saddle horses belonging to James and Luke had some "rough edges," the ones Jonas had selected to ride were definitely several shades on the "greener" side of greenbroke.

Eyeing them in the corral, James had inquired whether or not this might be the case?

"Greenbroke? Greenbroke?" Jonas had retorted in his clipped characteristic way. "What does that mean? There's no such thing as greenbroke. When somebody calls a horse greenbroke, that means he tried to ride him but he couldn't, that's all that means!"

And with that he led Luke's buckskin on up the loading chute and into the rickety old five-ton van with "Phantom 309" emblazoned on its sides. From within its dark interior, he barked orders to James and Luke to bring him the rest of the string.

There are, of course, many different methods of leading a terrified, half-wild bronc up a loading chute—all of which were unknown to Luke and James.

During the rodeo that followed, Jonas, in an uncharacteristically pessimistic aside to James' wife, declared: "I'd just as soon shoot myself as ride the Edson Trail with these two!"

But with Jonas, a deal was a deal, and the deal had been made. Southwest of Valleyview, back where the muskegs met the homesteads of today, they unloaded the horses late in the day.

⋆

Jonas' mood, which had been bordering on belligerence, especially towards Luke, but occasionally also James, had melted considerably when earlier in the day the "Phantom 309" had

73

more or less conked out going down the highway. Jonas, mumbling to himself, seemed to think it was something it "ate" and quickly prescribed and administered a dose of something he regarded as a sort of motor Alka-Seltzer vital to the inner workings of the old truck and in good supply behind the seat at all times. Luke, on the other hand, seemed to favour the idea that it was something the truck had "drank" and with little or no formalities, he had slid underneath and gone straight to work on the gas line. Jonas nearly tripped over Luke's long legs as he walked around to give the ignition another try. Instantly alarmed, he demanded to know what Luke was doing under there!

"Just pullin' off the gas line," was Luke's semi-distracted reply.

"How? You don't have any tools! Why?!"

"I got my knife," Luke had countered. His knife was more like a sabre that would have made Jim Bowie green with envy.

"I darn near threw a rope around his legs and jerked 'im out of there!" an almost gleeful Jonas had related to Doug over supper. He went on to tell how Luke had indeed discovered water in the fuel supply, how he had drained it off using only his knife and how the Phantom had come the rest of the way without skipping a beat.

Doug was a rancher in that country. He had some advice on where to begin looking for the first all-important landmarks. In fact, he'd begun making plans to join the expedition himself in a couple of days.

₊

The next day greeted the men with one of the most pleasant rarities of midsummer: brilliant sunshine combined with a cooling breeze.

The trio rode out in correspondingly high spirits with Jonas aboard a skittish young paint, James beside him on an eager young bay and Luke well behind them on the packhorse. Luke's buckskin was slightly lame. A small stone had wedged in the frog of his left front foot, bruising it slightly—nothing serious, but "Smoky" was a kind of pet to Luke anyway, and if he could spare him, why shouldn't he?

James and Jonas, never tiring of history, chatted as they rode, while Luke, the artist, seemed more content just taking in the various passing scenes (of which he himself was one of the more spectacular).

The packhorse was the only one who had refused to be influenced by the beautiful weather. He seemed to require almost constant prodding from Luke to maintain the pace set by Jonas and James. Unfortunately, the horse's mood seemed to infect Luke, who grew less and less cheerful the farther he lagged behind. Not that it was difficult going. They were riding the high sandy ridges that wound for miles through the muskegs. However, if it was true that the ridges were easy to ride, it was also true that they didn't lead anywhere.

Many a blind alley they were forced to abandon and their steps to retrace. On these returns, they would encounter Luke and his steed, who were now caught up in a bitter contest, each trying to out-belligerent the other.

These muskegs were not simply swamps or bogs a few hundred yards across. The spongy thatch of moss and peat and Labrador tea that formed the floating skin of the muskeg seemed to stretch for miles in all directions. Some kinds of muskeg, in some kinds of weather, will carry a horse, for a ways. Jonas and James had surmised that this wasn't one of those kinds.

At last they happened upon an old (from the 1940s perhaps) logging trail. Trails usually go someplace; perhaps this one led to the higher ground they were searching for where the remains of the "Moose Crik stopping place" were rumoured to be found.

Things were looking good when, in about an hour, the trail arched slowly upward onto a sandy hogback, covered in lodge-pole pine. Massive table top stumps, the remains of the giants logged off thirty years before, appeared here and there between their comparatively spindly descendants. The trail held and even grew stronger as it began to descend the hogback—an easy wagon trail by Jonas' reckoning. So when at the end of the sandy ridge the trail came to an equally abrupt end in the muskeg, the disappointment was matched by consternation at the failure of the most hopeful route they had found so far.

"Must have been a winter road," James suggested, but Jonas wasn't listening. He was gazing out over the hummocky expanse before them, arms folded atop his saddle horn. He appeared to be thinking.

"I don't like muskeg," he said eventually, as if in answer to an inner question.

About this time, Luke and the packhorse arrived and for the first time that day took the lead. Past Jonas and James they strode, Luke pestering and prodding all the way out onto the muskeg for about a hundred and twenty feet. Then the ground suddenly refused to support their weight any longer, and down they went. The horse sunk up to its chest, Luke nigh up to his, in the black mud now oozing up along the horse's sides. The animal had sunk to one side as it went down, pinning Luke's left leg against the thick skin of the muskeg.

Jonas looked on at Luke, squirming and kicking in an effort to free his leg from beneath the horse, which was doing its own considerable squirming and thrashing, and said, "Now, why do you suppose he did that?"

The pinto seemed to show visible signs of relief as Jonas turned it around and headed back the way they had come.

Luke finally did manage to extricate himself from the hole in the muskeg; but it took a lot of sweat and all the rope they had to free the packhorse.

Back in camp, Jonas had nothing further to say about the incident.

* ⋆ *

It rained that night, and the horses fought in the night and got tangled into a giant "cat's cradle" of halter shanks and picket line. The commotion had apparently not been enough to waken Jonas, so the boys had to wade into the mess without the benefit of his advice. In the morning, however, Jonas made a brief remark to the effect that they'd done "all right."

After a long rehash of the maps (modern topographical as well as some originals of the trail drawn in 1914), they decided to strike a new course a considerable distance north of where they had previously been. By mid-afternoon it had paid off. The three of them, Jonas in the lead, rode into a small clearing in a stand of poplar trees. The grass grows taller where once there stood a house, barn or shed. The foundations of several buildings of various sizes were marked by the taller, greener grass and sometimes a dished-out hollow. A passing forest fire had long since levelled all else.

Jonas rode to the centre of the clearing and dismounted. His pony grazed on the grass while he pointed out which buildings were which, where the corrals had been, and where "the Trail" had been. This had been a stopping place, a frontier hotel, an oasis for man and horse.

He told them about the old mountain man who ran the place and about the cauldron on the back of the stove always full of mulligan stew. He remembered that his mother and sister had got to sleep in a bed.

"This was the first place I heard Robert Service poetry," he said, and climbed back on the sorrel gelding he'd ridden out on that day. They rode back to camp silently, each bringing to life the scene Jonas had recounted to them.

James had known Jonas as a bronc rider, truck driver, boxer, rancher, teamster, horse trader and a variety of other things in that line, but his only known interest in the arts (namely his fiddle playing) had seemed to be a pecuniary thing. He'd strap his fiddle to a green bronc and ride to the dance on Saturday night. He'd get two dollars for playing the fiddle at the dance and a silver collection for flanking the bronc at the community picnic the next day. So, James was just a little surprised at the old cowboy's mention of poetry. He asked him about it at the campfire that night.

"Well," Jonas began, "we were sitting around the cabin not too late in the evening; the horses had bin fed and things squared away. We'd bin talkin', the grownups mostly, about this, that and the other thing, when the old fella that ran the place—still can't recall his name, but I remember his face—he looked at me and asked, 'did I like poetry?'

"I told him, 'Yes, I did. Some of it.' And he took a small volume down from the shelf, told us that the author was Robert Service—a man from the Yukon Territory, who worked in a bank—and then he read us some of it. I can remember one of the ones he read to this day."

Then, without hesitation, Jonas went on to recite, not just one poem, but several, without any apparent strain on his memory banks. Not all of them were by Robert Service. Many had introductions: "My sister's favourite was…," or "My mother always liked…" His father's favourite poem had been "A Touch of the Master's Hand." It was about a broken-down old fiddle brought to life by a "masterful old man."

There had been a special warmth around the campfire that night that the boys would harken back to in years to come.

* * *

Hard riding lay ahead. The Waskahigan River crossing seemed to be of some special importance to Jonas. It was also the logical "jumping-off" place for the boys. If they were to stand a chance in their bid to "ride the Edson Trail," that is, ride south from where they were to Edson following as closely as possible the original route of the now nearly invisible trail, they would need an authentic point to start from.

Doug had joined the party with Jean, his lady friend from the *Valley Views* newspaper.

Eliminating the many possible locations of the crossing had been work. When finally it boiled down to one last hope, things weren't getting any easier. The way down onto a wide U-shaped river flat presumed to be the site was blocked. The river had changed course, and the old riverbed had converted itself into a tangle of deadfall, marsh and weeds that a weasel would find difficult to cross, never mind a horse. The only high ground was a very high and narrow cliff along the downstream southern bank of the river. This high cutbank sloping down onto the flats would have served as the perfect "land bridge" to the flats, except for the fact that it was cut in half at the very top by a narrow crevice, created by a dry wash. A gap of fifteen or twenty feet made the difference. A drop of thirty or forty feet made them hesitate. Jonas wanted to go on.

Jean held Doug's horse while Doug made the arduous climb down to the bottom of the ravine and up the other side. When he got there, Jean threw him a rope. With Doug pulling on one end, and Jean thrashing and yelling on the other, the horse gathered up all its strength and leapt into the air.

Miraculously, when it came down on the other side, Doug was not under it.

Jean's horse seemed to be a little less confident in its jumping abilities, but after several attempts at dragging Doug into the gully and some extra prodding from James who had come to help, it too made the leap.

Jonas was next. He waited patiently for the way to clear. Jean was standing by, politely ready to aid Jonas in the business at hand. When his real intent became clear, despite her obvious respect for the man, her voice betrayed doubt as to the soundness of his judgement.

"You're not going to ride across!" she said.

"Why not?" he snapped.

"He might fall," she protested.

"If this horse is going down," he said, eyeing the chasm before them, "I'd much rather be on top of him than underneath him." He then ended the discussion with one quick jab of his spurs into the ribs of his pinto.

The horse took two jumps, the second being over the ravine, and landed on the other side without displaying any obvious knowledge of where it had been.

Inspired by this performance, James and his bay performed a similar feat. Luke and the packhorse, however, had seemed to feel the need to go back down the trail a ways and take a murderous run at the situation. Unfortunately, in so doing, they managed to get just a little off course so that when they came to land on the other side, there was only room for the packhorse to do so. He squeezed in between two stout willow trees, ejecting Luke up into the crown of one of them. His weight was enough to bend the willow out over the gully, and there he was left dangling in mid-air.

As Jonas turned his horse to progress down onto the flats, James heard him asking Doug, "Now, why do you suppose he did that?"

* * *

The five rode out onto the flats. Jonas led while the other four fanned out behind him. Feelings of suspense and expectation were very thick among them. Nobody was quite sure what they were looking for, but when Jonas reined in and sat gazing solemnly ahead, all knew he had found it.

They rode on several paces more. Here, one shelf dropped off about ten or fifteen feet to a lower one. Clearly visible between them was the narrow cut in the earth made for the wagon-wheeled traffic of the Edson Trail!

"Right there," Jonas said, pointing to the old road bed, "is where my sister and I upset the wagon. Over there," he went on, pointing to an ancient "bam tree" on the river bank, "there's where my mother and sister and younger brothers camped for nearly two weeks while my father and I rode on ahead to find a new tongue for the wagon. My sister and I had broken ours when we upset…"

His voice trailed off. He sat motionless for a moment or two, then with an almost imperceptible slackening in the reins, signalled his horse to walk and the two of them moved slowly on down the trail to the river.

Instinctively the other riders held back, allowing him to go on in silence.

When after a short time they felt it proper to rejoin him, they found him at "the crossing," gazing out over the river and into the high timber on the other side. His voice had regained its curt business-like tone as he launched into an impromptu lecture on the site and the traffic it had seen.

"The bridge was here," he said, and on the far bank, the remains of the ancient pilings could be seen. Sixty-three years before, a teenage Jonas had driven a team and wagon over this river, behind his father and mother aboard the wagon in the lead.

As he listened to Jonas describing the scene, it occurred to James that Jonas and his family had crossed that bridge never to return. Glancing around it would appear that no one, no one at all, had ever passed that way again—until today.

* * *

Now, that probably should have been the end of a happy story. But for Luke and James, the story, like the dread, was just beginning.

The trip thus far had been a success in every sense of the word. They had accomplished almost all goals and expectations that had been set for this part of it, and it had been pleasant, if not downright enjoyable, for all concerned. As cantankerous as he could be, Jonas did manage to orchestrate a flow and harmony to the events of a day. True, that flow was at times a trifle constricted, at other times a trifle too wide open, to suit the boys, but overall...it had been great!

In fact, a slight sadness came over them at the realization that Jonas and his friends were leaving them. This, mixed with the natural impatience to get on with the big trip, to be on their own, and...to get it over with.

They could not have had any specific foreknowledge of the conditions or events to come that could have given rise to dread. It may be unfair to impart an equal share of the foreboding to both James and Luke. If Luke felt it, he showed no outward sign of it. In fact, as in the muskeg a few days before, he seemed to display a general ignorance of fear in its various manifestations. Whatever he chose to do, or whatever chose to befall him, he applied himself to it with a singleness of mind that was enviable.

The dread, James decided, had to do with where they were going. While this wilderness, this nowhereness, had been home, workplace, playground and life itself to Jonas, it had a decidedly foreign quality to James (which total immersion would magnify many times).

He'd always taken the bush for granted—lived around it all his life—but seldom had he been at its mercy. He had been reared amidst the technological wonders of the post-war age. He and his generation had escaped nature and its tiresome truth and consequences. Armed with all the knowledge and know-how that can be gleaned from a library on the techniques of tying on a pack to a horse—the diamond-hitch, single diamond and double diamond—James and Luke managed to throw a pretty fair half-diamond. James climbed aboard his own horse to lead the results of their handiwork out for a test.

The packhorse was not at all hyperactive but when, after about ten paces, he suddenly realized that the rattling menace scraping the trees and flapping in the breeze was following him, he did what any horse in that kind of peril would do—he tried to outrun it!

James had casually looped a couple of wraps of the too-long rope around the saddle horn, and now, as the packhorse raced by and hit the end of his tether, those wraps tightened in a semi-permanent knot around the horn. Sensing that a race was in the offing, James' horse now bolted and easily passed the packhorse, still reeling from his arrival at the end of his rope.

About the time James was getting his saddle horse back under control, the packhorse was off again. This time he attempted to pass on the opposite side, pulling the rope around the rear end of James' horse and up under its tail. As a result, he didn't get quite as far as he had the first time before he hit the end of the rope. When he did, it was unanimously agreed that it was time for a general change of plans all around.

The packhorse decided that since he could not outrun this predicament, a bucking fit was in order. James' horse, with apparently no plan of its own, immediately decided to follow suit (as well as it could, at least, with the offending rope clamped tightly under its tail).

James was having trouble formulating a plan, or so it appeared to Luke. He watched from the ground where he lay rendered temporarily useless by paroxysms of uncontrollable laughter.

The amazing thing was that their half-diamond held tight through it all. There had been a great wealth of little lessons to be learned in this incident, and it wasn't long before the little party was headed down the trail, which they had discovered in the vicinity of the Waskahigan crossing. An old logging trail, like others they had seen, followed a course almost due south. It was likely that the loggers had adapted the then-visible road to Edson for their own purpose.

Unfortunately, this route was leading them into direct contact with one of the more legendary drawbacks to travel in that country. Up until now, and without really realizing it, they had been the benefactors of three coincidental factors working together on their behalf. First, they had never ventured too far from the breaking, cultivating, road-building and grazing of the local farmland; second, most of their meandering had taken place on high ground; and third, even when they did venture out into the flat lands and muskegs, they had enjoyed the presence of a stiff breeze.

Now they were penetrating deep bush, sheltered from most breezes and remote from any unnatural drainage. Bulldog flies half the size of a man's thumb (their bite leaves not only a welt but freely flowing blood) and smaller, endless varieties of horse-flies, fruitflies, sandflies, mooseflies and mosquitoes numbering in the millions all began to seem tame in comparison to that most penetrating and maddening little pest—the no-see-um.

James had cruised timber and worked on seismic. He thought he'd seen bugs. The packhorse took the worst of it. His black coat took on a grey sheen under the mass of crawling, shimmering insects.

When the men were loading him, they would have to be constantly slapping at his flanks with their hands to keep off the worst of the offending bane. Their hands and the ropes turned red from the blood. Even Luke began to feel sorry for the creature.

One morning, having finished packing the horse, they left him standing in a smudge (a fire built of logs and sticks and smothered with green leaves) they'd built specifically for his relief. Hearing a noise, James turned from where he was saddling his own horse and could scarcely believe the sight that met his eyes. The fire had dried out and finally overtaken its covering of green leaves, thereby greatly reducing the smoke and the protection it offered. The horse had then walked into the open flames and was dragging the coals out under his belly. Fortunately, the boys got to him before he had done anything worse than burn the hair off his fetlocks.

Nor were the men spared the effects of this pestilence. Their faces and hands began to swell from the constant and varied stings and this, combined with the more than audible drone of the clouds of tiny vampires, began to play on their nerves.

However, nature is not relentless. This is at times next to impossible to believe as one pokes along hour after hour in real and growing misery. But inevitably, the trail would break out along a wind-blown ridge where no insect flew. The sweat would dry on the horses' flanks and the men would breathe deep and exquisitely thankful sighs of relief.

It was just such a time the night they camped on the shores of a big backwater formed by a beaver dam. Both the horses and the men had eaten heartily. Nigh unto dark they were lying around enjoying the bug-free quality of the welcome breeze when, somewhere out across the water, a wolf pack set up a spine-tingling, magnificent howl—as if it had been their intention to entertain.

Then, slowly, the pack drifted off with intermittent howling marking its departure. Curiously, one lone voice, almost reluctantly it seemed, began to drift away from the rest and back in the direction whence they came. Closer and closer it came until the boys realized that, undeniably, it was headed for the spot where they lay.

On the opposite shore in the dying light, they struggled to make out its shape. The large form came into view loping along and leaping the occasional fallen tree or other obstacle it found in its way. It stopped to howl once more on the shore as it approached the camp, its motionless men reclining in the camp-fire light. The horses seemed amazingly indifferent to its approach. On it came until it broached the ring of firelight—and then sat down!

A young one, they thought, for although it was quite a con-siderable size, it still had a sort of puppiness about it—the more so as it cocked its head and gazed at the scene that had triggered its potentially fatal curiosity. Not that it had anything to fear from these fellows—nor was it likely that it would meet with anyone else, but elsewhere in the world, members of its species had died for much lesser crimes.

Then, perhaps because it had grown bored with the scene, its tawny form launched into the dark and away.

That night, ironically, James slept in peace, freed from the insects and the sense of foreboding doom that had plagued him along the way. But by noon the next day, both were back in full force.

Luke was riding along beside the packhorse when he sud-denly realized that he could not hear the hollow rattle of their tin pot. The billy can, which they found useful for packing water around camp and for boiling tea, was usually thrown up onto the top pack with a rope threaded through its handle.

They had just crossed a narrow creek. The alders hung in a low ceiling over the crossing, and when the packhorse had jumped the creek, he had driven the packs up into the alders—probably shearing off the pail on top.

They rode back to see. Sure enough, there in the mud on the edge of the creek was their pail, and right beside it, freshly stamped in the mud, was the biggest bear track they had ever seen.

Grizzly, undoubtedly, planted right on top of the tracks they had just made!

Luke stepped his size-twelve riding boot down into the track. It fit with at least an inch to spare before and behind.

"He probably wasn't following us," James opined. It was a natural crossing; all sorts of game used it. They mounted up and headed out with this comforting thought in mind.

But all comfort was drained from their minds, and the sweat stood out on their foreheads, when the horses balked a few minutes later. With their ears forward, eyes wide and nostrils flaring, all three refused to budge a step farther, although they all took turns volunteering to stampede backwards.

Cursing their mounts through gritted teeth and kicking all the way, the boys were finally successful in driving their horses beyond this mysteriously harrowing place. Once past, horses and men eagerly agreed to put it some distance behind them.

They had estimated that this day's march might land them at the site of the original "halfway house." In the days of the Edson Trail, it had been famous for its outdoor clay ovens. It was easy to understand in this muggy heat why a person wouldn't want to be baking bread indoors.

The place had been one of the biggest and most successful, providing a kind of intermission for trail-weary travellers completing the first major leg of their journey. Its remains, including the hay meadows, ovens and buildings, were rumoured to lie at the end of the trail the boys had been following.

* * *

In the airless heat and buzzing flies, no welcoming breeze greeted them as they broke out of the trees and onto the rim of a deep and narrow little valley.

James' sense of impending doom was reaching its zenith as they descended the narrow switchbacks. At the bottom, tired and thirsty, they found that the creek was dry.

Powdered silt, eroded from the logged-off sites upstream, choked its bottom from bank to bank. Something about its talc-like texture prompted James to acknowledge, in part, his pervading ill feelings, and he admonished Luke to test the crossing on foot before the horse tried.

Luke tied Smoky to a small drift log lying on the bank and strode out across the dusty bar. Reaching the other side, he glanced back just in time to see his four-legged pal decide to follow, dragging the drift pole by the reins as he came.

He hadn't quite reached the centre when, with only a small poof of dust as a warning, the whole creek bed seemed to cave in, virtually swallowing the horse in one huge, dry gulp.

In the melee that followed, it is hard to say exactly what took place. The cave-in created a sort of implosion first and then a kind of geyser made of dust. As that cleared, Luke was visible on the far side of the hole. He'd managed to grab Smoky's halter shank as the horse, his head and part of his neck protruding from the silt, flailed and lunged desperately against his would-be grave. With James and Luke on the rope and the horse seeming occasionally to find the bottom, they eventually began to make gains.

Panting on the bank, all three wore a thick coating of the dust, now mixed with their sweat, turning them all a greasy grey.

A quick check of the creek bed showed that the silt was continuous along its length. Lacking the heart to give it another try, and considering that it was now getting quite late in the day, they made the decision to camp there for the night.

The combined effects of the heat, the insects, the bear track and the dried-up creek dust lining their faces, began to take their toll. Not usually quarrelsome, Luke and James now seemed to argue over every little thing that came their way.

Smoky, for instance, his hide still covered in dried dust and sweat, provided numerous excuses for increasingly heated exchanges. Luke never tied him up, and therefore Smoky had the run of their camps and could pick and choose where to feed.

He was easy to catch—in fact, would usually come when Luke whistled or called, but he was a pest. He had mastered the art of opening the pack boxes with his teeth and would, if you let him, drag out one thing after another in search of the rolled oats at the bottom, not caring in the least what else he ruined along the way. Neither was he above stealing from the other horses. In fact, he seemed to prefer the oats allotted to them in favour of his own and could be quite a bully about it if they did not agree.

Begrudgingly, in deference to James' almost continuous complaints, Luke pieced together a few extra bits of rope and twine and sadly led his friend down the trail to be tied up.

Everything had been more work in that valley. It had taken the better part of an hour to locate a swampy little spring where the horses could drink. Grass was thin, so they'd had to be rotated around the place on their tethers.

Once, the packhorse had spooked at something, putting all their nerves on edge.

Grizzly, both men had thought as they watched the horse lunge and pull back and do everything but climb a tree.

The sky was overcast, but that didn't seem to bring down the heat. A storm was brewing and that brought out the flies and mosquitoes in swarms that were amazing to see.

They built smudges and smeared the dust of the poplar trees on their faces, but nothing gave relief.

Hoping to end their misery by sleeping, they rolled out their bedrolls at dusk and decided to forego the usual evening tea.

James could not sleep. He huddled under a light wool blanket to fend off the flies, cursing the no-see-ums that pricked the corners of his eyes and hating Luke for snoring blissfully on the far side of the fire, which had all but died.

An ear-piercing scream from the packhorse suddenly vaporized all these little woes and left James kneeling, supercharged with adrenaline, beside the dead fire staring wide-eyed into the coal-black dark of the overcast night. He'd never heard a horse make a sound like that, and for a moment he wasn't certain that he had heard it as he strained to see into the blackness.

There it came again, and the thought came to him all too clearly that he'd never heard a horse being carried off by a giant grizzly before. He reached over and gave Luke's shoulder a firm but quiet shake.

"Mmm…," murmured Luke, refusing to relinquish sleep.

"Luke, Luke! There's something down at the horses!" James said under his breath, giving Luke another, firmer, almost violent shake.

"What? What is it?" Luke asked sleepily.

Another scream from the packhorse answered his question.

"Holy lightnin'!" was all he could say as in one long continuous whirl of motion he rolled out, pulled on his boots, plunked on his hat and strapped on the bearhide holster (over the full-length red flannel underwear!).

It occurred to James that there was no sign of a scuffle in between the screams. He turned his attention to the remains of the fire in an effort to bring a flicker out of the coals and perhaps enough light to see.

The packhorse had been tethered in some thick willows, where he could rub off the flies and this fact, combined with the dark, rendered him invisible though not forty feet away.

One more cry of anguish was one too many for Luke, who raised his gun towards the sky and let fire.

The loud retort and the flash of the shot showed the packhorse rearing back on his tether.

Then silence. Now the real terror began to set in. Whatever it was should have stampeded at the sound of the gun.

A grizzly was the only animal James could imagine wouldn't spook at a situation like this. For the first time, he really began to believe that the bear looming there in the darkness would presently be charging—he thought of his horse and decided that he just had to see.

The first flicker of light, as he blew on the coals and offered them his handful of dry grass and twigs, brought an alarming sight. Luke was slowly levelling his gun in the direction of the screams.

"Don't shoot!" James called in a desperate plea.

"I'll just clear a few leaves out behind him," Luke answered, and pulled the trigger before James could protest again.

This time there was an answering sound as the creature began to flee. Indeed, the whole forest seemed to be coming down around them as a very large animal crashed through the dense night.

Following the sound with his eyes, Luke seemed to catch a glimpse of it as it crossed the trail to his right.

"Holy lightnin'! Holy lightnin'! It's as big as a horse!" he gleefully shouted in a tone more of amazement than relief.

James glanced down the trail in the opposite direction, partially visible now in the growing light.

"Where's your horse?" he asked the merry marksman.

The question hit Luke like a pail of cold water and, following the direction of James' gaze, he instantly went to investigate.

In a moment he was back with the answer in the form of a broken piece of twine in his hand. He was a shattered shell of the man who seconds earlier had presented such a portrait of jubilation in victory.

In fact, as he painfully repeated the obvious conclusion—"I shot my own frickin' horse, I shot my own frickin' horse"—he slowly sank to his knees.

Then, in a spirit of penance and self-flagellation that was quite terrible to see, he began slowly and purposefully pounding his head in the dust, repeating the agonized mantra, "I shot my own frickin' horse."

Was this funny? James began to wonder, in between the sobs of laughter that were slowly bringing him to his knees.

Thus the two carried on for an interlude of indeterminate length, one in the throes of agony, the other involuntarily in throes of the opposite extreme.

* * *

Early the next morning, Luke and a light rain roused James from his sleep. Luke had already saddled both horses, made tea, broke camp and stashed their things. James complied by hurrying through a token breakfast and they were off in search of Luke's buddy.

Though tracking the horse had not been easy by any means, and though Luke had not exactly been good company along the way, the scene of the two being reunited had been enough to bring a tear to even James' trail-hardened eye.

Luckily for Smoky, Luke's first shot, the warning shot, had been the slug. The birdshot could be seen liberally peppered over his buckskin rump as Luke and James came upon the horse in a hilltop meadow. From about the middle of his back and up from the knee on his right hind leg, dried streams of blood led to small round perforations in his hide.

Luke called to him once and his ears pricked up. Luke called a second time, and the horse came bounding over the meadow, apparently having totally forgiven Luke for what must have seemed harsh punishment.

On the way back to where they'd stashed their things, the painful decision had to be made. Smoky could not be saddled on top of those pellets, even though he betrayed only the slightest signs of stiffness or pain. Luke was ready to hike, but there was still the risk of an infection developing from those many wounds, and they had not brought any form of antibiotic. To go on was to risk the horse. They decided that James would ride on ahead to phone Jonas. James was, of course, faster on horse than Luke on foot, and this would give Jonas some lead-time.

Riding along by himself, James had begun to think of ways he could explain, or excuse, or…but he always seemed to come back to the simple and most direct way: "Luke shot his horse."

And he knew exactly what Jonas would say then: "Now, why do you suppose he did that?"

Never mind, thought James. If it had been a grizzly, how many men could have been depended on to stand their ground like that and fight? On the other hand, what kind of lunatic would fire a load of birdshot into a full-grown grizzly at close range?

He walked up to the farmhouse, dreading it all the way, and asked to use the phone. At least the smiling lady left him alone to make the call. He wouldn't have to watch her smile fade to fear and wonder as he explained.

Jonas answered the phone.

"Hi, it's me," said James.

"What happened?" Jonas asked in his clipped, pertinent way.

"Luke shot his horse," James said, and then fumbled on with something about "just winged him...bear in camp...dark..."

"Did he get the bear?" Jonas asked.

"No," James answered.

"Bear get the horse?"

"No," James answered again.

"Lucky," said Jonas. "Used to be pretty common, that sort of thing." And with that he dropped the subject and moved on to details concerning their rendezvous and horse hauling.

Sauntering back to where he'd tied his horse up in the shade, James felt strangely elated. "So that sort of thing used to happen all the time, eh?"

James began to breathe easier. He could feel the dread finally lifting. He'd once heard "the Trail" described as "the end of everything you'd ever been, and the beginning of everything you ever would be." For him, and for Luke, it had been a trail out the back door of time.

Dusty's Dream

man without a dream is like a book without a hero. In the oil patch today, for instance, the dream shared by all is no longer "a gusher"—that glorious event that takes place when a wildcat well suddenly erupts into a towering geyser of black crude!

From roughneck to tool push, from cat-skinner to camp-cook, the dream shared is a paycheque fat enough to sustain itself all the way to the next fat paycheque without dissipating in truck payments, bar bills, etc.

Not so, however, with the Brothers Bronson and their ram-rod father who together owned and operated Teamster Transfer, a trucking company specializing in the delivery of drilling mud to the rigs. The boys had a penchant for hard physical labour, which harkened back to their upbringing on the home ranch. The old man had a penchant for hard monetary policies concerning the local labour pool and suppliers. The upshot was that the Bronsons prospered beyond the paycheque into a world of investments, overseen by the patriarch, and prospered again.

And yet, even the fruits of the endless toil, as they continued to pack the hundred-pound sacks of drilling mud through the sweltering days of summer and the forty-below nights of winter, failed to instill in the boys the sense of having fulfilled a dream.

The two youngest boys, following the earlier dalliances of their father, gravitated to professional chuckwagon racing—which comes with a built-in dream of a championship.

The eldest, known as Bull, did not seem to have the yen for show business that goes with pro wagon racing and seemed at a loss for a personal vision. It came to him, and this may have constituted a flaw in the idea, in the form of an investment. Bull Bronson decided to get into the heavy horse business. Pulling competitions, the show ring, sleigh rides and horse logging were all bringing attention to this antiquated equine class and nobody, it seemed, was supplying this trend in an organized and studied fashion. Bull would corner the market!

* * *

The hay crop was bad that year, and the meat price on horse-flesh was down. Bull discovered that it was a buyers' market as he scanned the countryside from his mud truck, stopping to inquire wherever the big hayburners were in evidence.

He bought Belgians, Percherons and Fjords. He bought a load of oversized mustangs from the Indians out in the Pass. He bought out a man known as "the Clydesdale Man," including his silver-studded show harness with the scotch tops, and the big white fifth-wheel wagon that went with it.

One of the last holdouts had actually been close to home. Old Dustin Stetson—"Dusty" to his friends—had a matched team of Percherons that were as big as they were ancient.

Dusty was a man who had lived his life-long dream of prospering on the land—much of it behind a team of horses. From the day he had walked onto what he now referred to as "the

home quarter," each day had seen some part of that dream realized by his own two hands.

"What do ya want 'em for?" old Dusty would ask over a glass
of whiskey poured by the magnanimous Bull Bronson.

"Well, I'm just buyin' big horses," Bull would say, keeping his
cards close to his chest as horse traders do.

"The gelding's twenty-four and the mare's twenty-six; 'bout
all they can do any more is eat, although I will admit they're both
still pretty good at that."

Dusty looked suspicious.

"Oh, I might hook 'em just for show," Bull admitted. "You
know, a few turns around the home place there—I got that
silver-studded harness and that big white fifth wheel—they'd
show that outfit off pretty good, don't you think?"

"They might at that," Dusty would say, as if truly imagining
the spectacle. Finally he'd broken down. "But you gotta promise
me they're not for sale for meat nor harness to anybody else—if
I sell 'em to you, they die with you, and in their own good time!"

Bull had agreed.

"More money than brains," Dusty had said, shaking his head
at the sight of the team being trailered down the driveway to
their new home.

* * *

Bull was rapidly becoming a victim of his own success. If he
wasn't breaking up a fight between two giant studs over a corral
fence, he was in the breaking corral trying to teach some rangy
pachyderm to lead.

There was the endless toil of packing feed and the monu-
mental task of trimming the dinner plate–sized feet! It is back-
breaking work holding one quarter of a one-ton animal between
one's knees while clipping, carving and rasping the hoof into
shape. This gets more difficult, of course, when the horse objects.

Bull had singled out a pair of caramel-coloured Belgians
with white tails and manes. At five years old, they were almost
finished growing but just starting their education. One would be

lying—which perhaps their previous owner had been—if he said they were halter-broke.

He sat in the stall opposite the two, sweating and tending to the bumps and scrapes he'd sustained while catching, leading and tying the pair into their stall. They were prime product, just wanting a month or two of breaking, but their feet were in awful shape.

Bull knew the tricks of the farrier trade and it wasn't the danger, certainly not the toil, which put him off—it was the time. Time was rationed between the mud hauling, the horses and the million other things that seemed to snatch at his days.

To quiet these two to the point where you could comfortably curry them below the knees might…"take a week!" Bull said, venting his frustration out loud.

* * *

A Clyde mare, three stalls up, turned to stare back at him as she munched oats. Even she, as gentle and well-behaved as the breed is supposed to be, had been a problem. She'd come up lame with a piece of shale jammed into the frog of her right forefoot. It was in deep, and starting to infect and cause her pain.

He'd had to tranquillize her to get her to stand for the operation, but all had turned out fine. He was keeping her in for some residual antibiotics and she was enjoying the pampering.

Tranquillizers! There was still more than enough left to do these two chicken brains! Bull blushed a little at the thought of tranquillizing a horse to do its feet, but desperate times call for desperate measures.

In ten minutes he was sipping a cold beer and watching for the Belgians' heads to droop—a sure sign that the drug was taking effect. The one on the left went first. The horse shuffled its feet groggily one last time before stretching its neck and letting its head sag towards the floor.

Bull snatched up his tools and moved across the aisle.

"Whoa now…whoa…" he said as he moved in alongside the dozy workhorse.

But a major flaw in the technique became evident as Bull tried to lift the first big foot. Far from fighting his efforts, the animal seemed unaware of the fact that he was there.

"Foot! Foot!" Bull commanded as he tugged at the hair of the Belgian's fetlocks.

A contented groan came from the horse as if to say that it just couldn't be bothered.

Bull swore a long and angry series of oaths as he stared at the giant hooves now planted like pillars on the barn floor.

"Damn!" he said, emerging from the stall. He dropped the now useless nippers onto the work bench and, taking a pull from his beer, was suddenly distracted by the sight of an old meat cleaver hanging from its rusty hook on the wall behind the bench.

"I wonder…?" he said, taking a last pull on the beer as he reached for the cleaver. He felt the weight of the instrument in his hand. It was good steel.

But to chop at a horse's feet? Bull almost laughed out loud.

"But what if…?"

In minutes he was back in the stall with the cleaver in one hand and a ball peen hammer in the other. Squatting before the first horse he held the cleaver out over a splayed hoof. Careful to be far enough down the hoof to avoid cutting into the quick, he held the cleaver firmly and, raising the hammer, let fly with one mighty blow.

The horse didn't bat an eye, which was good because the cleaver was now firmly embedded across the toe of the hoof. Two more whacks with the hammer and the jagged overgrowth popped off, leaving a clean, straight edge.

The hammer and cleaver sang as the jagged chips flew. From one leg to the next Bull went until the first horse was done and he was on to the next. Ducking under the belly to the last two hooves, Bull wiped the sweat from his brow with the sleeve of his shirt. Five mighty whacks with the ball peen hammer and the front foot was done.

Such was the concentration with which he worked that Bull failed to notice a slight swaying from side to side on the part of the horse above him.

It was during the fourth or fifth whack to the last hoof that he was distracted by the sight of the hoof next to it slowly and rigidly lifting into the air. A great shadow passed over Bull as with a sudden sickening horror he realized that the animal was falling stiff-legged in his direction!

Bull was quick, but not quick enough. As he leapt upwards, he was struck by an avalanche of horseflesh pinning him against the timbers of the stall. Only his head and shoulders and one arm were left protruding above the caramel-coloured crush. He hadn't the breath to shout for help, though there was probably no one near enough to hear him anyway. In vain he slapped the hammer handle weakly against the horse's side. But the animal's brain did not register the signal, wrapped as it was in its chemical dream.

Somehow Bull managed to crook his right knee under himself, and gathering what strength he could, gave the first push upwards. His face and chest gained an inch towards freedom, sliding along the rough-hewn planks of the stall. His lungs strained to regain escaped air. It never occurred to Bull that he may well have expired there, but inch by inch, gasp by gasp, he gained the freedom of the concrete alley where on his hands and knees he did nothing but breathe for several minutes.

At the wheel of his mud truck the next day, cradling his bruised ribs, Bull began to think of advancing to the selling part of his plan sooner than he had foreseen.

In the meantime, the work of breaking the young teams to harness was much more rewarding. Here Bull borrowed a technique from the chuckwagon drivers. One simply hooks the beginners with experienced horses and heads down the racetrack.

Instead of the track, Bull had the open pasture in which he would attempt to steer a large arc. In one rather incongruous four-up, Bull had hooked the rangy young Belgians in the lead and Dusty's old Percherons on the pole. The Belgians had threatened to skid the old blacks along on their heels and would have, but for the superior weight of the blacks.

After two rugged circuits of the pasture, Bull noticed with dismay a slight wobble develop in the old mare's hindquarters.

"Git up, you grass-bellied old sow," he'd snarled from the box. But he cut short the last tour of the pasture and headed back to the barn.

Bull's dream, so it seems, had for some time been playing havoc with the dream of another.

Wendell Crane was a "back-to-the-land-er." A junior high school teacher by trade and a city-dweller by birth, Wendell dreamed of living off the land. He had secured a bush quarter within commuting distance to work. Slowly he had put in place the basic necessities of survival: power, running water and a modest mobile home—Wendell planned to replace the latter with a log house as soon as he could learn to build one.

The Crane farm, Wendell had decided, would be small scale and fully organic. And the land would be tilled, as up until a generation or two before it always had been, by horses. The fact that Wendell knew nothing about horses, much less farming with them, except what he had read, did not worry the man.

Sensibly, he had decided to start with a team of horses that had been fully trained, something safe, easy to drive and reliable. He didn't mind if he had to pay a little more and was forthright in explaining this to the various contacts he'd been given.

But it seemed there had been a rush on the supply of workhorses, as most of the suppliers he'd called were sold out. Several, however, had passed on the name of a man they knew could supply him: Bull Bronson.

Bull had understood very little of what Wendell Crane had said to him on the phone, but the words "don't mind paying more" stood out immediately.

"I got just what you need," Bull had responded.

"They're well trained?" Crane had enquired.

"Guaranteed!" Bull had answered confidently. "In fact, I'll even let you test drive 'em." And with that, a date was set for a viewing at Bull's place.

On the appointed day Bull was out early combing and brushing and harnessing Dusty's team. If Bull's conscience bothered him concerning the pact he had made with old Dusty, it was assuaged by the well-known fact that all is fair in love and war—and horse-trading.

The team stood dozing in the sun, resplendent in the silver-studded harness. They looked good. In fact, Bull called to his wife, who was working in the garden nearby, and asked her to be sure to take a snapshot or two before he unhooked.

Wendell arrived, equally resplendent in a brand-new pair of bib overalls and a starched white cowboy hat of the pressed straw variety. Bull couldn't help noticing, as he extended a welcoming handshake, that the man's palms were as white and clean as the hat.

"So this is the team?" Wendell asked affably.

"Ready to roll, just climb on up," said Bull, leading the way from the hub of the tall front wheel, to its steel rim, to the top of the box and finally, onto the elevated seat.

"Big wagon," Wendell commented as he gained his perch beside Bull. Together they gazed down upon the broad backs of the Percherons.

"They're fourteen and sixteen," Bull volunteered, thereby neatly shaving a decade off the truth.

"How long do horses live?" asked Wendell, voicing a natural curiosity.

"Oh, safe to say you'd get another ten years outa them," Bull answered, taking up the slack in the reins. "Git up!" he barked. "Git up!" he said again, slapping the lines against the big black rumps.

Slowly the pair lifted their heads and, picking up one foot and then another, headed in the direction of the driveway.

"Git up!" Bull barked with another slap of the reins and the team moved beyond their plodding pace to an even walk.

"What kind of feed do you have them on?" Crane asked brightly.

"Ahh…," Bull answered slowly, unsure of the point of the question. "Grass? 'n maybe a little grain er hay."

The big wheels rumbled past the house and on down the driveway, lined on both sides with young spruce trees. Glancing both ways to make sure no one was coming, Bull steered the outfit across the road, down into the ditch and into the open field on the other side. It was fresh summer fallow and the tugs came tight as the wagon cut deep into the loose earth.

"Git up there," Bull said with another slap of the reins.

"I suppose if you were working them hard all day it would be best to have them on grain," Wendell conjectured.

"Yah...oats," said the driver.

"Oats...," said Wendell thoughtfully. "Straight oats?"

But Bull was noticing with some consternation the return of the wobble he'd noticed in the mare's hind legs. He steered in a U-turn back towards the driveway.

"Here," he said, passing Wendell the reins. "You might as well drive."

"But, I haven't actually..."

"Nothin' to it," Bull drawled. "'Git up' means go and 'whoa' means stop."

Wendell sat bolt upright, a white-knuckled fist clamped around each taut rein as the big wagon dipped into the ditch and lurched up onto the gravel road.

"Give 'em a little more line," said Bull, and Wendell reached forward, leaning out over the front of the box.

Bull sat with his elbows on his knees, pondering the wobble. He was just on the verge of admitting to himself that it was quickly developing into a stagger, when he noticed his wife starting out from the house, camera in hand. He glanced back just in time to see the mare neatly cross her back legs in a futile attempt to maintain her balance before toppling to the ground beside her mate like a giant sack of beans.

Wendell was almost jerked out of the box on top of her as he sat frozen to the reins. In a flash, Bull had bailed out of the wagon onto the ground and onto the mare where, gripping the docile gelding's harness for balance, he began leaping as high as he could into the air and landing both heels as hard as he could into the great black mound of flesh just ahead of the mare's midriff.

His wife, emerging from the trees just in time to take in this rather novel scene, could be excused for not recognizing her husband's actions to be an attempt at CPR.

"Honey," she asked in amazement as Bull gave up the jumping and leaned on the gelding, "what did that horse do?" A pertinent question, really, given the extreme nature of the apparent punishment.

A single snort of laughter escaped the husband, answered by another as he turned to face Wendell Crane, still transfixed by what lay before him.

"Two for the price of one?" Bull asked.

With this short induction into the "School of Horses," it is thought that Crane decided on more extensive reading on the subject. For his part, Bronson decided to get out of the heavy horses, taking a net loss as he sold off the herd—all, that is, but the surviving member of Dusty's old team, which eventually died pleasantly in grass up to its knees.

The Convert

A cold sweat came over Harry James. "You go on ahead, I can handle him," he told his brother.

"I know I said I'd help ya, but if I don't get in and get them parts by six, I'll be shut down till Monday!" said Carl.

"No problem." Harry gave a careless shrug. He felt trapped.

"Why don't you wait 'til tomorrow?" Carl suggested.

"I'm here now," Harry said. His throat was drying out. He had imagined, almost without admitting it to himself, that Carl would do it. "I might as well go ahead," he said, with another shrug.

"Yah," Carl said with a twisted glint in his eye. "You better drive him first." The glint grew into a full-blown grin as he climbed into the pickup.

"Yah," Harry answered. He was suddenly glad that Carl was leaving; a strange blush of shame merged with heart-stopping fear as he watched the pickup drive out of sight. How had he gotten into this? The thought crossed his mind that Carl had planned it all along.

Over the last couple of years, Harry had taken a gradual but increasing interest in horses. A couple of day-rides at a friend's ranch had reintroduced the interest he had associated with childhood.

Up until that time, snowmobiles and other off-road vehicles had satisfied any residual urges he had had to get away from it all.

Carl, on the other hand, had developed his interests in horses and wilderness into a business guiding and outfitting big game hunters (with a little farming and custom horse-breaking on the side).

Harry was just beginning to take notice of his brother's accomplishments when he found himself expressing his own intentions to "get into horses again."

If this surprised Carl or any of a handful of friends they were sharing a drink with at the time, no one let on.

In fact, all in attendance hailed Harry's intentions with unanimous approval and an equally unanimous refilling of the glasses.

Whether it was the mood of acceptance generated by the cowboys' enthusiasm for Harry's ideas, or the positive atmosphere attributable to just the right number of drinks, one couldn't say, but for whatever reason Harry's enthusiasm was growing in leaps and bounds as was his confidence in his new-found opinions on the subject.

The talk had turned to a horse named Buck. Carl had been describing how two men on horseback and one on foot had worked for over an hour trying to catch the horse in a twenty-two-acre pasture, and how, in the end, they had resorted to snaring him with a lasso tied between two trees.

Harry had thought this a very poor practice and immediately made some very sound suggestions for future handling of the horse.

Buck's owner, who happened to be present, expressed a fascination with Harry's ideas but confessed a fear that the horse's needs went beyond his own capabilities as a handler.

Here Carl stepped in with a rather obvious suggestion, which in turn sparked a rather long bout of wrangling and haggling, the upshot of which was that Harry went home that night the proud new owner of Buck.

* ⭐ *

A squirrel jerked across the path and hysterically cursed Harry as he passed. Harry didn't notice. He walked the long walk of the condemned to the pump-house where Carl kept the tack. With a rope and halter in hand, a saddle blanket under one arm and the saddle hoisted onto his shoulder, he set out for the breaking corral with not one iota of courage or determination. He trudged on imagining Buck waiting for him with lots of both. His heartbeat stampeded.

Why had it gone on this long? When had he crossed the point of no return? He racked his brain for a way out but there just wasn't one.

The day they went to get Buck, even Carl had cursed the animal. It had taken the two of them most of an afternoon just to get a halter on him and load him. Right then he should have told the guy it was all a mistake and he could keep the horse. But he didn't tell him. He thanked him, shook hands and paid him—in cold, hard cash! For what?!

Harry had become a pretty good rider over the past couple of years. A horse crow-hopped for him once and another had reared. He'd had what he liked to describe as "a runaway aboard a mustang paint" but this was different. To climb onto a bronc that you know is going to try to kill you, with no idea as to how to prevent him from doing so, was nothing short of lunacy!

He'd told Carl that too. "I'm no bronc rider, Carl," he'd said. But Carl had said there was nothing to it. Harry insisted that he thought there was, but then Carl had told him there was nothing to be afraid of. Harry then told Carl that he wasn't afraid.

"Remember: a horse ain't tryin' to hurt ya," Carl said. "He's just buckin' cuz he's scared or cuz you're hurtin' him."

Then they had proceeded to tie the horse to the snubbin' post and scare the hay out of him with blankets and everything they could get their hands on.

It worked though because before long, moving in slow and gentle, they could pass a rope around his neck and he'd stand still for it.

A little while later, they even managed to get the saddle on him and then turned him loose in the corral. He bucked and pitched and sunfished until his flanks foamed with sweat, and the sweat stood out on Harry's forehead from watching him. Eventually though, he seemed to come to grips with the saddle and almost forgot he was wearing it.

The next day was the day to try some reins. For this Carl used the long lines from the wagon harness. There was panic all over again, but in a short while Carl was driving Buck around, "gee-hawing" him like an old plough horse.

"Nothin' left to do but git on 'im," Carl had chuckled.

But Carl was in town buying parts for the combine. Saturday, they had agreed, would be the big day.

"Traitor," Harry muttered as he threw the saddle and blanket over the top rail. He hung the halter and rope on a post and looked across the corral at Buck. Buck gazed back with a sleepy, uninterested air about him. He was a good-lookin' horse, Harry thought. With a yellow hide and white mane and tail, he almost looked like a horse Roy Rogers would ride.

"What can he do to me?" Harry wondered. He'd fallen off horses before, three or four times. He'd seen a horse fall on Carl once, and Carl had walked away from it with only two cracked ribs. That wouldn't be so bad.

The thought of walking into the office with bandaged ribs or a cast on his leg and a "my horse threw me" story appealed to Harry.

"Lunatic," he said out loud. To climb into that corral with the idea of breaking ribs? But he might not. Buck might not even buck.

"Carl, I don't want to ride him. Carl, I'm not going to ride him." It would be so simple. It would all be over if he could just bring himself to say these words—except that he would never hear the end of it. It would be all over if he could just bring himself to climb in there and get on him.

That blushing fear came over Harry again. He didn't belong here. An audible moan escaped his parched lips, but the adrenaline was starting to flow. He grabbed the halter and the rope, climbed over the corral and strode towards the horse.

Catching Buck was no problem. Harry slipped the rope gently around the horse's neck and tied it as Carl had instructed him. Getting the halter over the animal's nose had always been a fight, but today it seemed to Harry that Buck was almost helping.

With Buck tied to the snubbing post, Harry introduced the blanket, working it down the horse's neck and up onto the withers. The saddle came next; Harry pulled the right stirrup and rigging over the cantle and tossed it up onto the horse's back. But the horse shied, and the blanket and saddle fell to the ground.

The same thing happened with the second try. The third time, Harry held the horse's head with his left hand and, while talking to him, threw the saddle with his right. Again Buck dodged, and the saddle missed its mark.

Harry's right foot drove up into the horse's underbelly.

"Knothead cayuse," he muttered in a nervous rage. The horse trembled but this time stood his ground as the saddle landed squarely on his back.

Harry reached under for the cinch and looped the strap through the ring, but as the cinch began to tighten, Buck shied again. Horse and man spun 'round the snubbing post in a frantic scramble that Harry once again lost. The saddle slipped to the side, and finally onto the ground.

Harry felt like crying. If God had created the horse to serve Man, then why hadn't he told this bonehead about it?

Wiping the sweat from his brow, Harry went at it again. This time, Buck responded with a bare minimum of fidgeting, and Harry was able to cinch him tight. It only took a second to buckle the double-rigging, and suddenly they were ready.

"Nothin' left to do but git on 'im." Carl's words rang in Harry's ears. Buck stood waiting as Harry untied the rope.

The thing that Harry feared most was the possibility of getting a foot stuck in the stirrup. Then, too, there was nobody around to hold Buck's head while he got on. He wasn't going to turn back now.

Cautiously, he put a foot in the stirrup and applied some weight. No reaction. He repeated the test. Nothing. Buck seemed oblivious, almost bored.

Harry grabbed the saddle horn and swung up onto the hurricane deck. His other foot slipped neatly into the stirrup. Hands, legs, guts—everything shook as he sat there, waiting. Nothing happened. He pulled up the slack in the rope and touched Buck's sides with his heels. The horse seemed to very slowly sink. "He's sitting down!" Harry thought. The idea was too absurd to take. Harry kicked him, hard.

Straight into the air the horse jumped as if off a launching pad. The rider whipped back against his grip on the rope. Instinctively he laid back as they came down. Buck's feet only touched the ground and they were off again. This time, Harry could feel himself buckle forward; the rope was pulling him down!

"Keep his head up! Keep his head up!"

It was Carl! Harry pulled with all his might. He felt Buck give a little, and he laid back in the saddle to regain his balance.

The horse went up again. The rider pulled in the slack and they came down together. Buck went up again, twisting to the right, but Harry was ahead of him and compensated: he was doing it! He was really riding him down!

He heard Carl cheering somewhere far away, and then after a brief moment of weightlessness, the ground came up and smashed him full in the face. Something grazed his shoulder and he automatically rolled away. He couldn't breathe. His mouth seemed to be packed full of dirt.

He rolled again. A snort from Buck still dancing in the air brought him to his feet and he ran—smack into the rails.

"Harry!" He heard his name being called from far away; everything was so far away. His legs went rubbery and he began to feel himself sinking.

"Are you all right? Harry! Are you all right?"

Harry looked into Carl's face, then turned his head to spit. He wiped his mouth with the back of his hand and looked at the blood and mud left smeared across it.

"Yah, Carl," he said. "I'm all right."

Carl grinned. "I'll catch him up," he said, and strode out into the corral after Buck.

Harry spat again and sat up. Everything felt kind of jarred out of place as he staggered to his feet.

A warm thrill came over him as he watched Carl corner Buck on the far side of the corral. Harry knew what he was going to do differently this time.

Over the Bounding Manes

Crystal Cove Marina and Campsite" read the hand-lettered sign tacked to a tall spruce tree in view of the highway. A couple of miles of gravel would bring you to the narrow parkway leading down to the cove, which did not resemble a crystal so much as a bloodsucker hatchery. But the murky, algae-ridden water was also alive with pickerel, perch and northern pike, making it a popular attraction to the weekend angler. The ever-growing campsite complemented by the new dock, tackle shop and boat rentals added to the cove's viability.

In spring and fall it provided a base for Carl Erikson's big-game guiding operation, while in winter, his partner, Ram Luff, contracted their skidder out to local timber haulers.

"What?!" Carl's tone startled Ram, who had actually been quite satisfied with his initiative. The two were down at the boathouse planning their attack on the day over a coffee.

"I asked old Ghostkeeper to come over an' help us with the team around ten."

"What the hell for?"

The answer seemed obvious to Ram, but again his partner's tone seemed to imply that he was missing something. He went on the defensive.

"You said yourself he can drive a team backwards better than most guys can forwards."

Thomas Ghostkeeper lived across the cove and guided with Carl occasionally. He had never possessed a driver's licence, nor the skills or desire to get one, but still satisfied whatever transportation needs he had by team and wagon.

"We don't need to drive the team backwards," Carl countered sullenly. The team was actually a pair of pack animals out of Carl's guiding outfit.

"I never drove a team before," Ram stated flatly.

"Yah, well that team has never been drove before, so you won't be teaching each other any bad habits!" Carl went back to brooding over his coffee.

"You haven't drove wagons either, have you…much?" Ram's question was a delicate one.

"So what?!" Carl exploded. "Horses are horses—if you can break 'em to ride 'n pack, you can break 'em to pull a wagon; them two are ninety per cent there already!"

The partners planned to have the team replace the tractor, which was noisy and stank of diesel, pulling the farm wagon around the campsite on maintenance work and garbage pickup. Eventually they would offer wagon rides—in the winter ice-fishing season, sleigh rides—as an added Crystal Cove attraction.

"I just don't see," Ram said evenly, "what it can hurt to have a little advice on the subject."

"We don't have the time!" Carl protested. "We'll end up foolin' the whole day away with that old coot an' then drinkin' the night away to celebrate! We just need to get it outa the way and get on with what really needs to be done around here…besides," Carl muttered as an afterthought, "some things just don't require a mouthy witness."

"But the team…" Ram began.

"The team don't have a choice!" Carl said with finality. "I'll supply the brains; they can supply the horse power!"

With that Carl planted his coffee cup down firmly on the counter and turned and strode out onto the deck. It was getting on towards ten o'clock. Surveying the scene before him, Carl was suddenly struck by an idea.

An old wooden rowboat was swamped in the middle of the boat-launching ramp. Someone had run it aground and left it overnight to settle there. Its bow stood high and proud, but its stern was submerged. It weighed a ton and could not be bailed or overturned by hand. They'd have to get the tractor and pull it up on dry land—or, the idea struck Carl, get the horses to jerk it up there. Just harness them up, back 'em in, hook onto the bow and she's done—or such was the basic plan.

The team proved a little skittish under the harness. The rattling chains and blinders flapping, the britchin' under the tail and the belly bands; then too, it was difficult to get them to stand together, quietly—they kept shying away from each other's slap and rattle and click as the harness would tangle or slip, and cause yet another fuss or foul-up.

Finally, the leather and iron seemed to hang together, and the team moved out behind a vigilant Carl and an ever-ready Ram.

A couple of times, when something jerked or crashed, the team seemed ready to spook and would have dashed if not for the two men who were dug in on the lines behind and not ready to see their harness and team disappear.

A modicum of jockeying fore and aft left the two bays standing before the bow of the sunken craft. Carl climbed aboard and stood on the seat just back of the prow at ready, while Ram sneaked in behind the team and carefully hooked the tugs to the double-tree that was hooked securely with a logging chain and a steel pin to the bow of the boat.

"Got 'em!" said Ram and broke into a wide grin. There is a warmth and a rush of satisfaction that washes over someone who has laid considerable risk to rest. The boat was heavy, the chains were strong, and do what they might, the horses could not now escape the task at hand.

A little less satisfied was Carl, who more closely represented a portrait of concentration mixed with caution, although he too, with the tugs hooked, seemed to abandon fear.

Bracing one foot against the side of the boat for balance, Carl took up the slack in the lines and, with one last backward glance at the enormous load that a half-sunken fourteen-foot boat represents, brought the lines down hard with a crack.

The horses, of course, exploded like two dynamite caps, charging the harness with uncoordinated no-holds-barred leaps into the air. Again and again, with eyes rolled back, they launched themselves into terror-stricken flight, only to be jerked back by the logging chain.

Carl knew enough of the teamster's art to know that a horse does not exert efficient force by charging the harness and bit. Its strengths are actually exerted in the almost cat-like actions of its front and hind quarters as it drops and pulls. This action, it seemed, must be learned!

However, such was the weight, size and desperation of the two bays that, jerk by jerk, the boat began to inch its way up onto dry land.

The almost imperceptible movement greatly encouraged Carl, who had almost been ready to conclude that the load was beyond their capabilities. He responded with renewed vigour in the slapping of the reins department, while Ram began bellering as encouraging a series of oaths and threats as one might expect to hear from the sidelines in any good fight to the death.

The team responded with renewed desperation, rearing occasionally and falling into their collars from standing positions. On these occasions, the corresponding jerks on the boat resulted in gains of a foot or two at a time.

With victory in sight, Ram added a random sampling of whistles and war whoops, and the boat jerked clear of the high water mark.

The bow now rested high enough to effect a dumping action over the stern. The load was lightening considerably, and a scant two or three yards more was all that was needed to complete the first task attempted by team and teamster alike. The bellering abated and the charging of the harness seemed to lose some of its vigour. But as the group neared the victorious end of their common chore, events began to take a rather unexpected turn.

* ⋆ *

The boat, now almost clear of the water and therefore high-centred on its keel, rocked over onto its port side. The water sloshed first to starboard and then to port, splashing over the gunwales in one solid wave the length of the boat. Carl, taken off guard by the sudden mobility of his perch, lurched to keep his balance, inadvertently slacking off on the reins just as the wave smacked out onto the ramp.

The sound of large waves striking concrete in the vicinity of their heels, it turns out, is a sound horses are unaccustomed to. In fact, the splash on this occasion was foreign enough to both horses to bring them together and of one mind to determine their best course of action for the first time in the exercise.

They spooked, firing like two overheated steam locomotives! The result of their renewed inspiration, combined with the fact that their load was by now very much lighter, was that the boat skidded up the ramp behind the horses at a slick pace. The scraping growl it gave off, as the keel gouged the gravel strewn over the ramp, seemed to convince the team further that they were in danger of losing their lives, tails first!

Carl, having regained his balance and bracing both feet against the bow, began screaming "Whoa, whoa…" in a tone as equally life-threatening as the sound of the boat scraping over the ramp, but to no avail.

The team clearly had the upper hand and they seemed to know it as they left the ramp. But the faster they ran, the faster they were chased. The panic that now gripped the horses made their early performance look like a bout of equine hiccups.

Bits in teeth, eyes ablaze, foam-flanked and terrible, this awesome "two-in-hand" charged past the boat rental shack, through the parking lot and onto the parkway that led past the camping stalls.

Ram, who back at the ramp had been inspired to lay hands on the stern in an attempt to slow the unscheduled departure, had eventually come to the realization that he was not going to win this impromptu tug-of-war. He'd had just enough time to bail in before the resurrected craft was planing through the dust of the parkway, headed for the gravel road at breakneck speed.

The timing was perfect. If only a few seconds later, the whole event would have ended in a collision between Adolphus Ghostkeeper's old Ford pickup and the runaway rowboat. Thomas Ghostkeeper had apparently convinced his brother that the project might prove interesting and the brother had agreed to provide their transportation.

He was not disappointed. Indeed, he had only time to hit the brakes before taking in what amounted to a spectacle unique to his many years around horses and boats.

Carl only just glimpsed the smiling face of Thomas Ghostkeeper as he blasted past him screaming "Whoa!" and pulling on the reins (as much for balance in an effort to keep "afloat" as in any real hope of stopping the thing).

When they crossed the road in front of the pickup, it was without pause to consider what lay ahead. They had emerged from the parkway and rocketed across the road and into the ditch on the other side. On that side, the team charged up a small embankment oblivious to the "acroboatics" the rowboat was accomplishing behind.

Ram had been trying to work his way forward to assist on the reins, but hadn't made it further than mid-ship when their course erupted into the ups and downs of the ditch. Miraculously, he stayed aboard, as did Carl, but somewhere over the brow of the ditch, the boat capsized, snapping the cleats that held the logging chain fast to the bow and setting the runaway team free.

When the dust began to settle, the Ghostkeepers ascertained that Ram had been thrown some distance into the field. Scraped and bruised, but otherwise none the worse for wear, Ram joined in the efforts to solve the mystery concerning Carl's whereabouts.

After some speculation and head-scratching, Thomas went over to the boat lying upside down and motioned to the other two to help him lift it. There, lying on his back, arms folded on his chest, lay the indignant remains of the "I'll-supply-the-brains; they'll-supply-the-horsepower" Carl.

Thomas, smiling his enigmatic smile, looked down at the man he'd discovered under the boat. He then looked out across the field to where the team was disappearing into the bush at the field's edge.

Glancing back at the man on the ground, he asked, "Where are you goin' with the boat anyhow?"

The Lightning Bar Gang

orseshit," Hank grumbled, and tossed the newspaper onto the kitchen table in disgust. The headlines spun down the arborite, coming to rest within view of Sal, who stood at the stove patiently stirring a pot of chicken noodle soup. She glanced at the newspaper and then at her husband, who had discarded his greasy ball cap and was running his fingers through his matted hair as if it hurt.

"What is?" Sal asked, watching the wooden spoon trail slowly through the noodles.

"Ahh, them horses," Hank said, as if it tired him out just speaking of the subject.

The soup came to a boil. Hank drew back as Sally approached with the steaming pot and ladled him a bowlful. As she filled her own bowl and set the pot back on the stove, Hank reached for a bologna sandwich, which he dunked in the soup. Sal sat up to the table and pulled the newspaper over beside her bowl.

"That's some picture," she mused, gently blowing the sting off a spoonful of noodles.

"Morons," Hank mumbled. The big buck teeth and gaping eye sockets leered out of the foreground while the parched hide remaining on the neck and bleached ribs stretched off into the background.

"Definitely died of something," Sal said.

Hank reached for another sandwich. "Wolves, old age? Nothin' lives forever. 'Bout the only thing it couldn't have died of is starvation!"

"How can you tell?" Sal asked, glancing back at the rack of bones in the picture.

"I seen 'em, remember?" Hank paused to dunk the last of the sandwich. "Back in March, when you'd expect them to be showin' off their ribs a little—an' they were hog-rollin' fat! They were in better shape than ours!"

Sal looked thoughtful. "But it has been dry—you said yourself the grass is burning up."

"Yeah, our grass is. The grass in the open pastureland is—but wild horses don't give a damn about that. They just move on to greener pickin's." He plucked a toothpick from a box on the table. "The meadows back in the high timber and the alder swales aren't done yet. And them native grasses hold a lot higher protein content anyway. I'll tell ya," he said, waving the toothpick for emphasis. "By the time the wild ones are dyin' of starvation in the middle of summer, the rest of us will already be in too much trouble to care!"

Sally was scanning the newspaper again. "Doesn't say where they took the picture."

Hank shrugged. "Coulda bin out at that big lick above Stony Lake—more likely right on the Grazing Association community pasture. Them type a' reporters aren't likely to stray too far off the roads."

The conversation drifted to the latest cattle prices, thistles and an upcoming wedding in the neighbourhood before Hank drifted back out to work on a new piece of fence line. Sal straightened things up in the kitchen and then set about the eternal chore of bookkeeping.

Once again pondering the age-old question "How is it that the bills always arrive before the cheques," she was suddenly distracted by the dogs heralding the arrival of a visitor. Sal didn't recognize the small white car coasting to a halt amidst the canine swarm. Neither did she recognize the driver. Sally watched from the kitchen window as the woman removed her sunglasses and put on a floppy white canvas hat with a pull string that hung under her chin. She emerged from the vehicle holding her arms and elbows out of reach of the inquisitive muzzles surrounding her.

"Good dog, good dog," she said repeatedly, without sounding sure of the fact. Sal took in the sight of the approaching woman wearing a dazzling white safari-style jacket, matching slacks and bulky hiking boots that were protruding from her pressed cuffs. The woman cast an inquiring glance at the house and began wading gingerly through the waves of wagging tails and wet noses.

When Sal stepped through the front door, the stranger hailed her as one would a passerby. "Excuse me?" she said. "I wonder if you can help me; I'm looking for the Davis ranch."

"This is the Davis ranch," Sal said.

"Henry Davis?" the woman asked.

"That's right," said Sal.

"Wonderful!" the woman said, and spontaneously her knees began bumping through the dog pack. "Is he here?"

"He's in the neighbourhood," Sal answered.

"Will he be back soon?"

"Fairly soon; would you like to step inside?" Sal pushed the door wide in a welcoming gesture while raising the other hand as a gesture of warning to the dogs that began bickering among themselves as they fell away from the stranger.

Inside, Sal automatically ushered the woman to a chair at the kitchen table and began assembling the percolator. "Can I get you a coffee?"

"That would be great," the woman said, taking stock of the room. "De-caf, if you have it."

"Afraid not," Sal said, setting out cups, sugar bowl and a plate of homemade oatmeal cookies. The coffee began to perk as she took her place opposite the stranger at the table. "I'm Mrs. Davis."

"Right," said the woman. "I'm Ashley Haiste—I have a card I'll leave with you. How do you do?" Ashley had snapped her business card onto the table and extended a formal handshake.

"Sally," Sal said, as they shook mechanically.

"I'm with the W.H.A." said Ashley. "You've probably read about us in the newspaper?"

"The W.H.A.?" Sally had picked up the business card.

"The Wild Horse Association. It's based in Calgary, but we have members all over the province—all over western Canada, in fact."

"What do you do?"

"What do I do?" Ashley sounded a bit defensive.

"The W.H.A." Sal clarified.

"Oh, right. The Association operates the 'adopt a wild horse' program as well as promoting general wild horse awareness and—"

"Adopt? A wild horse?" Sal seemed to be asking if she had heard the woman correctly.

"Yeah, I know, it sounds a bit...different, but..."

"It sounds," Sal said, rising to tend to the coffee, "like a contradiction."

"Not really," Ashley said as the scalding coffee filled her cup to the brim.

"Assuming," Sal continued, "that by 'adopt' you mean round up and take home."

The woman went on to carefully explain that the W.H.A. was all for the preservation of wild horses in their natural surroundings, but that when the animals were threatened by habitat loss, unscrupulous hunters, or nature itself, the Association stepped in to see that they were well taken care of.

"And the herd that ranges south of us here? Are they to be 'taken care of'?" Sal looked at the woman over the brim of her coffee cup.

"Well," began Ashley, who did not meet Sal's even gaze. "As you are probably aware, that herd is facing starvation."

"No," said Sal as if suddenly interested. "I wasn't aware of that."

Ashley brightened considerably as she went on to review the recent newspaper coverage in lurid detail. She grew almost ecstatic as she outlined the yet-to-be-released plans for a roundup of the herd and its subsequent dissemination among members of the W.H.A.

"And you think you want to talk to Hank about this?"

"Who?" Ashley asked.

"My husband, Henry Davis," said Sal.

"Oh yes, Mr. Davis, of course," enthused Ashley. "In fact, we'd like his help."

"His help?" Sally's tone betrayed amazement.

"Well, not with the actual roundup necessarily. Our members usually volunteer in good numbers for that. But as a guide—to help us locate the herd and familiarize our president and head wrangler, Will Stanton, with the area."

"Help locate the herd," Sal echoed as if deep in thought.

"Of course we wouldn't expect him to do it for free!"

"No," Sal agreed matter-of-factly.

"If he could give us an estimate of what his guiding fees would be, based on his day rate or a contract price, I'm sure we could easily come to an agreement."

"An agreement," Sal echoed.

"Do you think he'll be much longer?" asked Ashley.

"I think he could be a while," said Sal gravely.

With that, Ashley gathered herself up, explaining that she had several courtesy calls to make informing "key locals" of the W.H.A.'s plans. "We find it politic to include the people in the immediate area," Ashley enthused.

"I can imagine," Sally agreed.

"I'll try Mr. Davis again soon—or he can call me on my cell— we'd like to move on this as quickly as possible."

Sal assured Ms. Haiste that she would be hearing from Mr. Davis on the subject and watched the woman disappear down the driveway in a cloud of dust and dogs.

* ⋆ *

Supper was steaming on the back of the stove by the time Hank came in, and it was on the table by the time he'd washed up. But it wasn't until the supper things were cleared away and the smoke rose above his favourite chair that Sally brought up the subject of the wild horses.

"I guess they're planning to round up those horses."

"Sounds like it," Hank said.

"Is that legal?" Sal asked, suddenly angry.

"Basically," Hank sighed, "feral horses aren't classified as wildlife, so any running free like that are fair game—as long as they're not wearin' somebody's brand."

"Where did they come from?" Sal seemed to be looking for loopholes. "I mean originally."

"Well," Hank began, "I guess you could say they're all that's left of an old-timer by the name of Tom Shakes. His cabin and some corrals are still standing; still a half-day's ride from the end of the world. Anyway, the story goes that he spent his days riding the eastern slopes down into the States and trailin' back the best-blooded stock he could find."

"You mean steal," Sal clarified.

"Well, Tom used to joke that all a man needed to make a living was a long rope and a fast horse—and some say he had a couple of bullet holes in his back to show that the horse wasn't always fast enough. But the fact is, he managed to raise some pretty respectable stock out there…and then one day, this was some years ago now, Vern Berbeck rode by the cabin and found 'im face down at the breakfast table. The herd's bin runnin' free ever since."

"They want you to help round them up," Sal said quietly.

"What?"

"In fact, they want to hire you."

"Who does?"

"There was a woman here today who says they'll pay guiding rates."

"In a pig's eye!" Hank looked cornered.

122

"Can't you just go out there and run them off?"

"Damn rights I'll run them off!" Hank said, looking dangerous.

"I mean the horses. Can't you just get them out of sight for a while?"

"Out of sight where? They were out of sight!"

"There must be some place." Sal was hoping against hope.

"Horses leave tracks."

"Catch them yourself!"

"I don't want 'em caught!"

"Then you can let them go again when the dust settles."

"It's not that simple." Hank seemed to be in agony. "Once you start feedin' 'em they don't always go back to grubbin' for themselves. You'd have to shoot that stud for sure."

"Maybe they won't be able to catch them?" Sal asked with scant hope.

"They'll catch them; you get enough guys together and it's no big deal."

"Well then," said Sal, "you might as well take their money—we could use it."

"That'll be the day!" Hank looked defeated.

"Take me out there."

"What?"

"I want to see them—you see them all the time, but I don't— I'd just like to see them, wild."

"When?"

"Tomorrow. We can get up early—do you think you could find them in a day?"

"Maybe," Hank said begrudgingly. "Maybe two."

"We'll take some camping stuff. C'mon, Hank." Sal was firm. "We haven't had a holiday all summer—let's just go."

Hank was looking at Sal as if he hadn't seen her for a long while, when the phone rang. It was Vern Berbeck, who had obviously received his visit from Ashley Haiste and was calling to let off steam.

"I know, Vern," Hank kept saying. "Yeah, I guess she was out here too…no, they were fine the last time I looked." Hank was looking at Sally again. "Yeah, actually the wife and I were thinking about taking a ride down there tomorrow…we'll look 'em over anyway…yeah, I'll drop by." He hung up the phone.

"Why not?" he said. "Pay our respects one last time."

⋆ ⋆ ⋆

They were in the saddle by the morning's early light. They had trailered the horses down to the community pasture and set out from there on an old logging road that eventually led down to the river.

They hadn't gone a quarter mile when they came upon the carcass. It was on a grassy knoll fifty feet from the road. Hank stopped and Sal followed his gaze to the discovery. "What did I tell you?" he said dryly, and spurred his horse up the bank. The big bay grew skittish at the lingering smell and tried to sidestep the thing, but Hank spurred it again and drew up inches away. Sal drew up on her pinto gelding a little behind Hank to find him studying the bones and hide intently. After another moment or two, he leaned back in the saddle.

"Well, it isn't a wolf kill, and it didn't die of old age."

"How can you tell?" Sal asked, studying the remains herself.

"Wolves would have scattered the bones more'n that, and by the look of those teeth it wasn't older 'n six or seven."

"So what, then?"

Hank shrugged. "Worms, mebbe. They can pick up bloodworm and things grazing behind domestic stock down here on the lease."

"I didn't know worms could do this," said Sal.

"If they're not treated—a horse gets wormy enough it wastes away…no matter how much it gets to eat."

A shadow seemed to pass over Hank's gaze. "We'll see what the rest of 'em look like."

The river was down. They crossed the ford with no problem, barely getting their boots wet. Creases of sweat began to show on the horses' necks as they climbed the steep switchbacks on the other side.

Hank paused to give the animals a blow. "It's gonna be a hot one," he said, leaning his elbow on the saddle horn and gazing into the valley. The river was as blue as the cloudless sky as it wound its way through the deep green of the forested valley.

"Git up," Hank said, and they resumed their climb.

Somewhere near the valley rim he turned onto a broad game trail that led off to the east. The trail soon became a maze as it forked through spruce thickets and rose over dry ridges. At times it disappeared altogether and they seemed to be travelling aimlessly. Hank rode silently at a steady, even pace, occasionally leaning out of the saddle to scrutinize the ground passing beneath.

Sal understood his silent ways when travelling in the bush. She felt no urge to fill the air with chit-chat, absorbing instead the scolding of the squirrels amidst the hubbub of birdsong or the distant cracking of a twig betraying the presence of a larger animal as it caught their scent. She noted the excavated anthills a bear had left. A buck mule deer, with eyes as black as eight-balls, paused to stare at them in disbelief before vanishing like smoke behind the veil of passing trees.

A trail no wider than the horses' feet wound through devil's club and wild roses under a canopy of giant poplars. The trail widened as it merged with others and widened again on game trails converging into a virtual game highway.

Sal, scrutinizing the ground for hoofmarks, found them in abundance, but only those of the cloven variety. The only horses to have passed this way lately were their own.

The bush became silent as they approached the lick. Even the horses grew wary as they caught the scent of the most recent visitors to the place. All the animals, it seemed, must visit these springs in search of the salts and minerals in the water. Logically, any place frequented by cougars and wolves would be a place where all would approach carefully.

The sun was hot as Hank and Sal emerged from the cover of the trees onto the baked clay surrounding the springs. It was lunchtime. They tied the horses under lodgepole pines a distance back from the lick, pouring out oats from the saddlebags before taking up their own picnic spot on a shady outcropping overlooking their surroundings. Whiskey jacks materialized like feathered shadows in the branches above.

The springs themselves consisted of two or three tiny rivulets glistening in the sun as they creased the surface of a pancake of clay about the size of an average front lawn in the city. Sal asked Hank about the bleached bones that littered the clay.

"That's a soap hole," he explained. "If you were to take a good enough run at it, you might make it halfway."

"And then?" Sal asked.

"An' then you'd break through the skin on top into the slimy grey muck underneath—which has no bottom—and, that's the last we'd hear of ya."

"So, the bones…?" Sal prompted.

"The bones are what's left of game that blunders in too far to get out and not far enough to sink. Whatever's stuck on top the scavengers pick clean." He tossed a piece of bread crust to the patient jays.

They left the lick on a trail that angled steadily upward until, topping a long ridge, they were greeted by a cooling breeze. Hank pressed on, quickening the pace. The spaces between the trees widened as the ridge narrowed, arching higher and higher into the blue sky.

Eight hours in the saddle, Sal mused. Eight hours was enough to let people forget their lives in captivity; lives that simply equated to hours, which equated to days, which equated to dollars. She thought of the man Tom Shakes who had lived his life at one with these hills and valleys. She looked at Hank riding straight and tall and wished they could simply ride on, living by the dictates of the sun, the wind and the rain.

The trail came out onto a promontory, and for a long while they sat abreast, silently scanning the scene. Below them was Stony Lake, nestled in high timber. To the east, the valley floor opened in a chain of marshy meadows, and opposite the meadows a long hogback stretched out parallel to the one they were riding along.

"Shakes' old place is just the other side of that hill," Hank said quietly. The ears came up on Sal's pinto. Hank's bay suddenly gave a whinny and looked as though it expected an answering call from the lake. Hank too was listening. "C'mon," he said. The bay wheeled and Sal followed at a gallop for two hundred yards down the ridge to where the trail suddenly disappeared over the side. Sal reined in, watching the dust boil up around the bay's flanks as it skidded downward before taking the plunge herself. The pinto skied, straight-legged in the front quarters and crouched behind, onto a shelf that they traversed to the next slide.

At the bottom, Hank turned in the saddle to see if Sal and the pinto were still upright, and finding them hard on his heels, was off again. They raced down the trail, ducking limbs and jumping logs before turning onto an old cutline that ran into the high tim-ber abreast of the lake. Here, Hank slowed to a trot and then to a walk. At one point he stopped altogether, listening over the sound of their mounts still catching their breath.

As he slacked the reins signalling the bay to move forward, he absent-mindedly reached down to give a tug on his .308. The rifle moved freely in its scabbard.

The forest floor was cool and dark. Mast-like spruce and pine towered above them, while molten shafts of sunlight slanted down-ward, blinding the eye to all else. They moved silently over the soft mossy ground.

A ruffed grouse exploded into flight a step or two ahead of the bay, igniting the nerves of horses and riders alike. Hank cursed under his breath and urged his mount forward.

Sal thought she heard brush break in the distance. The pinto nickered. The bay stopped, wide-eyed and ears forward, and lifted its head to neigh—but Hank cut it short with a jab of his spurs and drew the .308.

The pinto suddenly wheeled and would have bolted but for Sal, both hands on the reins. The bay was champing at the bit, rigid and quivering under Hank's firm hand. In his other hand, he held the rifle butted against his hip as he scanned the dark wall of trees.

Suddenly Sal could see them! A single file of six, maybe eight, horses led by a dapple-grey mare running ghost-like through the gloom of the forest. Off to the left, another column led by a pinto with a long white mane. As their trails converged, the white mare leading the first column laid back her ears and flashed her teeth at the leaders of the second, sending them into disarray.

A big bay, two or three back in the line, did a forced jump of a deadfall, which lay in a patch of sunlight, flying out of sight into the relative gloom again. Twenty, maybe thirty horses were now in motion on the forest floor as Sal, calculating their direction, realized with a sudden thrill that they would cross the cutline not two hundred yards from her and Hank.

Mares, colts, yearlings—where was the stud, the legendary lightning bolt stud?! A dark sorrel with light mane and tail, named for the fact that early in its life a bear or a snag had ripped it open from the base of one ear, down its neck and over its shoulder to its leg—the scar had grown back white, resembling a lightning bolt.

A squeal of rage close at hand answered her question, sending her pinto into a spin it took all of her strength to contain. Hank, holding the bay, jacked a shell into the chamber of the rifle, training its open sights on the ribcage of the stallion as it pawed the air menacingly. It squealed again, openly challenging the trespassers, then tossing its head and unkempt mane, turned to race down upon the stragglers of the herd as they streamed through the sun on the cutline.

Moments later, a distant whinny echoed through the pines…they had vanished.

Hank let out a long sigh as if he'd been holding his breath, ejected the shell from the chamber, and turned to Sal who, like her pinto, sat silently staring after the herd.

"Well?" he said with a broad grin. "Whaddya think? They looked pretty healthy to me."

"They were magnificent!" she said. "That stallion is the most amazing animal I've ever seen!"

Hank's laugh rang out like the peal of a bell. "He's one for the books all right—great shape too; they all are—all smooth and nice."

"Magnificent," Sal echoed. She didn't know whether she wanted to laugh or cry.

They decided to ride over to the old Shakes place to camp for the night. Finding the cabin sound and dry, but occupied by an anti-social pack rat, they elected to sleep under the stars.

Hank seemed more interested in the corrals, which were also found to be in fair shape. He dug a ball of old binder twine out of the camping supplies and after a half-hour spent tying up rails, turned their horses in on the high grass of the largest.

On the way over from the lake, he'd shot a grouse, which he now turned on a spit while Sal made bannock and warmed up a can of beans. They sipped tea in the twilight, reclining together against a big pine stump on the banks of the lazy creek.

"Would you really shoot that stud?" Sal asked thoughtfully.

"If I had to…," Hank said. "He survives by what he can do with them hooves and teeth—if a person was to push their luck, it would soon come down to a him or me situation."

"Is there any way they can round up the others without destroying him?" Sal was growing wistful.

"Well, if it was me," said Hank, "I'd bring down some irresistible young filly and bait him into a good high pen someplace out of the way."

"Would that work?" Sal asked hopefully.

"No reason why not," Hank said. "A little extra work, a little luck—it should be almost easy."

Nighthawks sang above them. Fireflies came out and danced along the warm clay banks of the trickling creek.

"Tomorrow," Hank said, "I'll get ya to drop me and the horses off at Vern's. When you get home, phone that woman and tell 'er I'll take the job—tell 'er a thousand bucks cash in advance, or cheque as long as it's certified, and I guarantee to show 'em the herd."

"When?" Sal sounded resigned.

"Tell 'em I need a coupla days to scout out the situation—three or four maybe—after that we can go anytime she likes." He reached out and drew the canvas tarp over them as they slid comfortably into their bedrolls and gently off to sleep. Sal dreamt of flying horses.

* ⋆ *

She did not need to phone Ashley Haiste when she got home. She met the woman coming out of their driveway just as Sal was turning in. Ashley was overjoyed at the news that Hank would be taking the contract and that he was already on the job. The W.H.A., it seemed, was anxious to move given the urgent nature of the situation; that is, given that the herd was perceived to be starving to death as they spoke.

Hank's required "three or four days" would mean the roundup could start on the weekend, which Ashley declared to be "Perfect!" Sal's kitchen table became control central as the outgoing and incoming calls and calls waiting blurred into endless chatter, notations and confirmations.

The community pasture was to act as a sort of base camp or staging area. The members would be arriving throughout the day Saturday and ready to ride Sunday. Will Stanton, president and head wrangler, would be arriving Friday in hopes of taking an exploratory ride with Hank early Saturday.

Sal reminded Ashley of Hank's cash-in-advance terms—standard in the guiding business. Ashley assured Sal that she would have a certified cheque for the full amount in hand by Friday. Sal agreed to try and get word to Hank concerning Mr. Stanton's desire to see the herd Saturday. And Ashley left, finally.

Sal called Vern's to find that Hank had already returned to the bush and that Vern had gone with him. What, exactly, they were up to, Vern's wife Cathy didn't know, but she voiced her suspicions openly in saying that whatever it was likely involved more than one bottle of whiskey. She said her boys were riding down there with a couple of neighbours the next day and would take the message concerning Hank's Saturday appointment to him without fail.

The next day, Sal got a call from Cathy with a message from Hank. He wanted her to pick him and the horses up down at the community pasture Saturday afternoon. Cathy said she still had no idea what was going on.

"They're corralling the lightning bolt stud," Sal thought, but kept it to herself.

Saturday came and with it a strange mood of expectation mixed with foreboding. In the mid-afternoon, Sal hooked up the trailer and drove down to the pasture.

A growing hamlet of motorhomes and holiday trailers, chrome-encrusted pickup trucks and horse trailers, glistened in the sun. Cowboys and cowgirls, as clean as the chrome, sprawling in lawn chairs or milling about in the din of competing stereos, looked up to greet Sal as the latest arrival. Her pickup was the same colour as the dust that wafted up around the rusted old stock trailer rattling behind.

Sal scanned the crowd for Ashley who, true to her word, had delivered the cheque the day before. She noticed a man shouldering a large video camera emblazoned with the logos of a television network. His subject was Ashley, resplendent in a teal blue cowboy hat and outfit to match that included a jade-studded belt buckle the size of a Viking shield. Sal was wearing the same jeans she'd worn to clean the barn that morning and one of Hank's old work shirts tied at the navel.

Ashley spied her and, having concluded the interview, came bustling over. "Welcome to the wild horse roundup!" she said, and bubbled on, rejoicing in everything from the weather to the turnout. Sal gathered that Hank had indeed made the rendezvous and that he and Stanton had ridden out early to see if they could locate the herd.

"So tomorrow we get down to work," said Ashley, sounding like she was still being interviewed.

"Did Hank say when they'd be back?" Sal asked.

"He said mid-afternoon, so it's what—it's now past four—but surely you're not leaving, you can't leave, we'll get some steaks on here in a bit, you know you're more than welcome to ride…"

"This looks like them coming now," Sal said. She was looking off to the distant southeast corner of the pastureland to where two riders had just emerged from the bush.

"Wonderful!" exclaimed Ashley.

"Jump in," said Sal, levering the pickup into first gear as Ashley bounded gleefully around to the passenger side.

Sal and Hank exchanged glances as the truck rolled to a stop, but Sal could make out nothing from his expression.

Ashley was out of the truck before it stopped. "Did you find them?"

"We found them, all right," said a tall man on a tall black Thoroughbred—obviously Will Stanton.

"Wonderful!" cried Ashley. Hank was stepping down.

"Will, this is my wife Sally—Sal, Will Stanton."

"Pleased to meet you," said Stanton.

"And you," said Sal.

"How do they look—are they in pretty bad shape?" Ashley seemed to sense that all was not well.

"They looked pretty good to me," said Hank, leading the bay towards the trailer.

"They look fine," said Stanton.

"Well, that's wonderful—I wasn't sure we'd made it in time," Ashley confided to Sal.

"Well, we didn't, actually," Stanton said with a tired smile.

It was clear that Ashley had grown weary of guessing. "What's wrong with them?"

"Somebody's bin writin' on 'em," Hank called out from behind the trailer and slammed the door shut behind the bay.

"What did he say?" demanded Ashley.

"They're branded," Stanton said.

"What do you mean, they're branded?" Ashley asked in a hollow voice.

"He means they're wearin' somebody's brand," said Hank, striding towards them. He reached his right hand up towards the man on horseback. "Will, nice ridin' with ya."

"You too," said Stanton as they shook.

"Ashley?" Hank said, extending his hand. "Nice meetin' ya."

"Nice meeting you," Ashley said limply, shaking Hank's hand. "You must have found the wrong ones," she protested. "I mean, they must be somebody else's horses."

"Afraid there ain't nobody else out there to have horses," said Hank. "Not out there," he added, climbing into the pickup.

"Drop by any time Ashley, Mr. Stanton," said Sal, nodding a farewell as she engaged the clutch. She steered a wide arc back towards the camper village to see that a reception committee had begun drifting out on horseback or by pickup truck. "Whose brand?" Sal asked.

"Not ours!" said Hank, grinning cheerfully as he waved to a passing pair of riders. "In fact, it's nobody's," he said more thoughtfully. "Vern made it up." He looked at Sal mischievously. "The Bar L brand—the L stands for lightning."

"Perfect!" Sal said, and laughed. They both waved to the happy passengers of a pickup that had pulled off the trail to let them pass.

"Vern's waitin' for us up at his place—yer pinto's there too— one of his kids rode it out last night."

"What about the stud?" Sal asked gravely.

"Oh, he's fine!" laughed Hank. "He's got a new girlfriend."

"Did ya see them?" shouted a passing horseman affably.

"You bet," Hank answered, and waved, smiling.

"The Lightning Bar Gang," Sal said wryly.

They looked at each other and smiled. It had been a good week.

Tinker

I first noticed him down in the park by the river. We were playing for a children's day camp. There were hordes of children of various ages attended by a handful of harried parks-and-recreation types. The only other person in the park was him.

We were all relatively young as well—the oldest being the bass player at twenty-two and the youngest a fourteen-year-old girl who sang and played guitar. There were eleven of us: actors, musicians, writers and technicians, on a summer tour. We rode together in a big blue bus and camped in whatever accommodations could be found. Upon arriving in a town we would play out a seemingly endless series of public service and publicity appearances building towards whatever theatre or concert dates had brought us there. This town was Drumheller, Alberta. The month was July, and the desert valley was living up to its reputation as a summer hot spot.

We played acoustically for the pack of kids in the park—that is, we used no amplifiers or microphones. Some danced and shouted, some laughed and sang (some wrestled and fought or threatened to escape)—while the old guy wearing a blue windbreaker over a yellowing white shirt stood in the shade of a giant cottonwood, smoking and listening.

A couple of days later I noticed him again. It was even hotter playing on the street downtown. A new recreation facility was having its official opening and our music added to the festivities. Part of the complex was a senior citizen drop-in centre and we had made our musical selections accordingly. Though dated, the tunes were upbeat, befitting the nature of the celebration. The crowd on the street seemed to be having fun—we were having fun—and I spotted the blue windbreaker leaning up against a red brick wall in the shade of a nearby alley, smoking and listening. Somehow the man's presence gave me a vaguely uncomfortable feeling as if he was auditioning us for something. It was absurd, but I found myself looking in his direction occasionally for some indication as to how we were doing. He gave no outward sign of approval or disapproval, beyond his attentiveness. The last time I glanced up, he had vanished.

Saturday night was our last night in town. It was an early show and the plan was to pack up immediately after and drive through the night towards the next town.

The hall had not sold out but what they lacked in numbers the audience more than made up for with enthusiasm. The company was exhilarated as they went about their various chores packing up the costumes and props and making the bus ready for the open road. I was not surprised to see him, although I was certain I had not seen him in the audience. He was wearing the same blue windbreaker as he stood chatting with one of the people who had been instrumental in bringing us to town.

I resolved that I would meet the man but returning from the bus to the last place I had seen him, I was disappointed to see that he had once again disappeared. Spotting the person the man had been chatting with, I was about to approach her to ask after his identity when she bustled over to me with the news that the entire company had been invited to a late dinner on our way out of town. While it was not uncommon for us to meet and enjoy the hospitality of new friends along the way, it was not all that common, given our numbers, that somebody actually offered to feed the lot of us. Neither could the offer have been more timely, as sandwiches and lukewarm Cokes in transit, while adequate, failed to compare with the offer of a hot meal!

*　*　*

The address was obscure—someplace out of town up the valley—as was the exact identity of our benefactor. I thought of the blue windbreaker, but in the general hubbub and last-minute details of gathering things together, had no opportunity to explore the subject further. We were given to know that the invitation constituted something of a novelty not to be missed—indeed the lady who had passed us the invitation now offered to ride with us as guide. I observed her eager anticipation of the event as she nestled in among us and began reciting directions to the driver. It seemed the woman had not actually been to the place herself although she was sure of the location. An air of notoriety seemed to lurk in her references to the place.

The sun was hanging low over the Badlands as we drove the valley floor in the general direction of some of its more famous landmarks. The swinging bridge—a footbridge suspended high over the lazy Red Deer River—the hoodoos further on.

"This is it," the woman said of a right turn off the pavement. The bus rumbled onto a winding gravel road leading into a narrow canyon. "We cross eleven bridges in only seven miles," she said, "or maybe it's only five miles—but I know it's eleven bridges for sure," she confirmed, and we all began counting them.

The woman had referred to our ultimate destination as a hotel but as the bus dusted its way over the narrow road, this became more and more difficult to visualize. The hills and mesas stretching to the canyon rim began to glow hot pink in the tangerine light of sunset. The baked clay of the canyon seemed to host the odd tumbled-down string of barbed wire leading to lonely looking farmsteads and ranch gates here and there.

"Nine!" a chorus of bridge counters gaily shouted as the tires bumped up onto the deck of yet another span over the dry creek bottom below. When at last our destination swung into view, the bus grew silent in awe of our surroundings. Before us lay the old ramshackle hotel painted an impossible baby blue. It fairly glowed in the ethereal light of sunset while up the canyon the other buildings, large and small, showed no sign of ever having seen paint of any colour. Tumbleweeds gathered in forgotten streets pocked with fresh mounds of gopher holes. The big blue bus coasted up to the big blue hotel and for a moment no one seemed sure of what to do.

"They're here," a voice rang out as the door to the bar swung open framing the sentry in the warm incandescent light within. We filed off the bus, instinctively snatching up a guitar here and a fiddle case there, and walked into the room. Although there had been only one, or maybe two, tired-looking old pickup trucks parked outside, the place was packed. We stood for a moment blinking stupidly at the smiles blazing back at us from all directions—many of them missing teeth or altogether tooth-less.

"Welcome!" cried the man behind the bar whom I recognized, despite his change of costume, to be the mysterious man in the blue windbreaker. The jacket had been replaced by a sort of admiral's uniform complete with a veritable spaghetti of gold braid and shoulder flashes. His name was Lawrence, and he was later to explain that he held the coveted position of Civil Defence Coordinator for the town and that the uniform went with the title.

"Come in! Come in!" he said, and in minutes the eleven of us, and our guide, were absorbed into the midst of the assembled personnel. Lawrence seemed to have been the youngest person in the place up until our arrival. It was as if the ghosts of the town had gathered in honour of Saturday night. Somehow we were being given the unimaginable privilege of joining this party—and what a party! The music was non-stop, and everyone in the room was rapt with lewd and boisterous song. A gaunt-looking old dandy, wearing garters to hold up his shirtsleeves, manned the piano that was perched on a low platform at the far end of the bar. Several of the ladies wore satins and lace reminiscent of the dance hall attire of old. In attendance were the famous bobcat twins—twin brothers who over the many years of their lives together had maintained the practice of drinking together and, once drunk, fighting each other. The hilarity seemed only to escalate.

A shuffleboard of the same elderly vintage as everything else in the room stood against the back wall. In one of the gutters at the end nearest the bar lay a cat. It was an uncommonly large cat, said to be pregnant at the time in fact, but otherwise a normal house cat except for its entirely uncommon passion for, or some would say addiction to, the game of shuffleboard. Indeed, it seemed to hog the table—a fact indignantly noted by Lawrence, the host and manager of the bar. However, the regular patrons seemed not to mind the animal monopolizing the game and would place the cat's rocks within its easy reach on the board. The cat would then place a paw upon its rock and with a surprisingly precise and studied action send the rock on its way down the board to the takeout or counting position it desired. The cat's opponent would then take his turn politely setting up the cat's next shot, and so the game would go as if it were the most natural thing in the world.

Lawrence saw to it that all in our company were served steaming bowls of homemade stew and frosty bottles of cold beer—all on the house. He had, perhaps in view of the underagedness of some of our troupe or the fact that the serving of beer and general mayhem was to go on well after legal hours, decided to lock the front door.

Lawrence had a telescoping arm with a hand on it with which he could solicit tips or tone down an overly obstreperous patron, but as I think of it I do not recall the cash register keeping pace with the flow of beer at all. This was rumoured on the floor of the bar to have something to do with Lawrence not actually owning the business himself. The owner, or so the gossip went, was said to be the elderly lady known to be the purveyor of the very excellent stew.

As I have said, the front door had been locked early on. There was, however, a back door left open wide onto the wilds of the darkened valley beyond. It afforded no cooling breeze, as the Drumheller valley seems not to cool off at night. Rather, the hills seem to radiate like clay ovens the heat absorbed by day from the sun.

Such was the general spirit and decorum of the place that I scarcely took notice when a horse strolled in through the back door and began mingling among the guests. Neither did any of the locals take particular notice, outside of greeting the animal by name—"Tinker."

Tinker was not a particularly large horse, and was pure white—in fact his long tail and shaggy mane had a silvery, almost translucent quality. I don't know how long he had been visiting from table to table, slowly making his way through the crowded bar, before I noticed that Tinker was mooching drinks at each table he came to. The animal had a technique of clasping the end of a beer bottle delicately between his front teeth then lifting the bottle aloft and draining its contents in one long and apparently enjoyable draft. He would then pause a moment before opening his teeth to let the bottle drop, whereupon the accommodating patron who had provided the beverage would catch the empty and the horse would set about mooching the next one. Few could object, considering that most of us seemed to be moochers as well. In fact, it was Lawrence himself, when someone failed to catch an empty that smashed onto the floor, who suddenly looked up from the bar in an obvious attitude of displeasure.

"You again!" he roared, and the horse gave a sudden start. "How many have you had?"

Tinker, having regained his composure, calmly turned towards the bartender, the picture of innocence, and attempted to stare the man down. It had been the only disturbance to mar the evening so far and the place went suddenly quiet in response.

"I said," Lawrence glowered at the offending patron, "how many have you had?"

For a moment the poor animal seemed to look away feeling the embarrassment of being put on the spot, then plucking up every residual ounce of dignity within, proudly raised his head and his right front foot and stamped it loudly on the floor. He then looked hopefully, and perhaps a little too quickly, back at the irate manager.

Lawrence folded his arms across his chest and sneered, "How many?"

The horse, obviously feeling cornered, lowered his head once again, picked up his front foot once again and stamped twice.

"How many!?" Lawrence bellowed, obviously in no mood to be trifled with.

Tinker caved in, pathetically lifting his foot and commenced to "Stamp, stamp, stamp, stamp, stamp, stamp" out the actual, and quite large, number.

"Out!" Lawrence barked, pointing the way in no uncertain terms, while the regulars, with the rest of us quickly joining in, began protesting on the animal's behalf.

"No damn way!" Lawrence yelled, shouting down the protesters. "You know what he gets like! The guy can't hold his liquor! Literally!"

The protests sounded again, fractured by laughter across the bar, as Lawrence, pushing from behind, evicted the four-legged dipsomaniac physically—the horse taking advantage of beers proffered on the way by those in sympathy with a horse after their own hearts.

And so the night went on: the music ebbed and flowed, the cat played shuffleboard, Tinker came and went, the laughter was continuous. As the first streaks of dawn stretched over the canyon, a kangaroo court was formed to hear a charge of "irrelevance" brought against Lawrence, as Civil Defence Coordinator of the town.

Our stage manager was appointed judge. Lawrence acted in his own defence, and as the case raged on, produced and read documentation showing that the position was his by prime-ministerial appointment. This was shouted down, by the jury, as being totally irrelevant, and for proof they offered several notorious examples of obviously irrelevant prime-ministerial appointees—not the least of which was the national Senate!

In the end, the defendant offered a summation that he played on a harmonica cupped in an empty beer glass. The verdict, as others joined in with voice and guitar, went in his favour.

By the time the big blue bus slowly backed away from the big blue hotel, its occupants waving fond farewells to those who had come out to see them off, a bond had been formed. It was as though the torch of true western hospitality had been passed with a trust that somehow the tradition would be carried on.

* ⋆ *

Time passed, as it will, and in a few years I found myself holidaying among relatives in and about Calgary and making the introductions to my new wife, Lynne. In fact, we were scheduled to depart from my Aunt Phyll and Uncle Bert's farm near Standard, into the drylands northeast of there, and end up at Castor where Lynne's family were. Scanning the route in my mind, I was suddenly struck by the fact that we were to pass precariously close to the Drumheller valley and the canyon that I had not seen since that eventful Saturday night.

I had told Lynne little about the place, depending instead on the beauty of the setting and the spirits that inhabited it to justify the unscheduled stop. As we wound our way through the heat of the canyon over the eleven bridges, my sense of anticipation grew into a feeling of homecoming. But as the big hotel swung into view, I was unsettled by the sight of two large white cube vans backed up to the front door.

As we parked abreast of one of them, I recognized the name of a prominent Calgary antique dealer on the door. Walking past the two men who stood amidst a litter of bedsteads, tables and chests of drawers, I realized, with a sinking feeling, that the two were engaged in a bitter argument over who had purchased what in a recent sale.

Stepping into the bar I was disturbed further by the sight of two workmen industriously nailing a veneer of cheap wallboard

over the existing walls. A bank of vending machines and electronic games now glittered and beeped where the shuffleboard
had been. There was no sign of the cat. Indeed, the only possible
remnant of the place I had known was a gaunt-looking pair of
elderly gentlemen, who were also the only customers in the
place. They sat in the far corner, next to where the stage had
been, sullenly nursing a glass of draft each. We chose a table in
their vicinity and sat down to wait. In due course a very busy
young man materialized from a door behind the bar and sight-
ing new customers, was immediately at our side.

"How are you today?" he asked brightly, adding, "What can I
get you?" without pausing for an answer to the first question. We
each ordered a beer. "Anything else?" the man asked affably,
planting the beers in front of us. I paid him and he disappeared,
squirrel-like, through his door behind the bar.

Lynne sipped her beer patiently while gazing about with an
air of mild curiosity.

The two older fellows had not said a word, even to each
other, since we had entered. Turning to them with a friendly
smile, I offered, "This place has sure changed."

They looked at each other, one of them "harrumphed" in
disgust, and then they looked back at me as if I was an uninvited
visitor from a different planet.

"Where's Lawrence?" I asked, taking a chance.

The two exchanged another glance and then turned their
gaze back on me.

"You from around here?" one of them asked suspiciously.

"Not really," I answered honestly.

"How'd you know Lawrence?" the other demanded.

When I told them that I had only known the man as bartender
there and added, "and Civil Defence Coordinator," something
clicked and we were soon exchanging memories of better days.

They invited us to join them and when the squirrelly young
man made his next appearance I ordered a round of beer,
thereby cementing the relationship.

They informed us that the place had indeed been sold and
that Lawrence had taken up with a "religious widow down in

Drum." It was even rumoured, they said with some gravity, that the man was now known to sing in church occasionally.

"What about Tinker?" I asked, and their spirits seemed to sink to a new low. For a moment I feared he might have died as I scanned the expressions behind the grey stubble. One of them raised his watery old eyes to meet mine and gave it to me straight.

"Bought by a guy up the valley," he said, "a tee-totaller." Pausing to let the gravity of the situation sink in, and choking back his own personal grief, the second one added, "That horse hasn't had a drink all summer!"

I was moved…I don't know how to explain it exactly, but seldom had I felt such complete empathy for my fellow man— or in this case, horse—as I did sharing this news, and a growing number of beers, with the two old gentlemen.

"You'd think somebody would have bought him a beer for old time's sake," I chimed in.

"It's been tried," said the one glumly.

"Tried?" I asked.

"The guy won't let ya!" he said, voicing his moral outrage.

"Well, what if we just forgot to ask him?" I said, starting to get my back up.

They both shook their heads.

"Won't work. He'd catch ya," they said in turn.

"Do you mean to tell me this guy actually stands guard over his pasture on the lookout for people trying to get his horse drunk?"

"Damn rights! You'd better believe it!" they said together.

"That's ridiculous!" I said, unable to quite picture the situation in my mind.

A discussion ensued where the old boys gave the lay of the land and a profile of Tinker's new digs.

"The horse pasture is off the back of the barn," said the one. "The barn is right off the main yard, opposite the shop; the house is just above both of 'em," continued the other. "The pasture butts right up against the wall of the canyon and except for a few dips and dives, you can see the whole thing from the yard."

"Any trees?" I asked. "Yeah," he said, "one—an old cotton-wood about four-fifths dead."

"There must be a way," I said. "Look, this guy doesn't know us. Maybe we could keep 'im busy while you two take Tinker a beer?"

"Might work," said the old fellow thoughtfully.

"What are you talking about?"

My wife, who had been presumed to be a silent partner in the discussions so far, was breaking her silence.

"If you knew this horse…," I began.

"If I knew this horse, would I feel the need to go out in the pasture and get drunk with it?" she interrupted.

"Well," I said, "not get drunk together exactly, but certainly have a few beers together." It sounded perfectly reasonable to me and the two sitting opposite us nodding their heads in unison.

I could tell she wasn't completely sold on the idea, but the mission was building up its own head of steam. I felt she'd come to see the altruistic side of the venture eventually.

"I'm not getting out of the car," she said, and I could tell there would be no negotiating on this point.

"That's fine," I agreed, and it was also agreed, in view of the number of planning beers consumed by myself and our partners, that she should drive.

"I'll get a case of beer," I said, rising. "Better make it two," said one of the old fellows, and the other nodded wisely.

With that we were off, our guides giving directions from the back seat, Lynne and I taking in the passing desert scenery from the front. In minutes, we were nearing our destination.

"Pull over!" one old fellow said as we crested a knoll over-looking what lay ahead. The road dipped into a sharp narrow gully, then rose in a winding course to Tinker's new home. It was exactly as the two had described it. The house, barn and shop were laid out in a triangle occupying a high point of ground overlooking the canyon. The horse pasture stretched out over the baked ground behind the barn and there, standing in the sparse shade of the "four-fifths dead cottonwood," head down, was the pasture's sole occupant, Tinker.

Tinker

* * *

Looking back at the farmyard, we could make out a tractor parked between the barn and shop. Its missing front wheel came rolling out of the darkened shop door, guided by the "tee-totaller" himself!

Something in me had believed that somehow the fellow just wouldn't be home and we would be left with the run of the place to pursue the joyous reunion. But it was obvious, as we watched the figure in the yard stooping over his task, that the man would be there for some time.

"What if we drop you two off in the coulee?" I said. "You should be able to make your way into the pasture up that draw."

They nodded in agreement. "The barn'll hide you halfway across the pasture or better—d'ya think Tinker will come to you?"

"Not unless we hollered for him," said the one. "He'd hear us first," said the other, indicating the farmer at work in his yard.

"Well, I'll time it so as to arrive in the yard when you're ready to go the last part of the way," I said confidently.

With that, we directed our driver to move on out, and the car coasted quietly out of sight into the bottom of the coulee. Once there, I looked at the two in the back grimly clutching a case of beer each and gave a nod. They bailed out either side, each admonishing the other not to slam the doors, which they pressed closed quietly, and, taking a last cautious glance around them, set off up the draw like two old coyotes. At the top they paused to peek over the edge, scanning the ground ahead. Liking what they saw, apparently, they clambered on up and over, disappearing on the other side.

Up until now I had not had much of a chance to consider what exactly my own role in the exercise would be. As we started up the road I decided that I would depend on the tradition of farmers' long-suffering approach to helping lost travellers.

We rolled into the yard and I stepped out confidently with a friendly smile. The tee-totaller didn't look up from his work on the tractor tire.

"Trouble?" I asked sympathetically.

145

"Just a flat tire," he said, reaching for the tire iron, and added, "What can I do for you?"

"Well, I'm just a little lost…," I began.

"You must be," he interrupted, still without looking up from his work.

"I'm looking for my uncle's place—maybe you know him? J.A. Milbak?" I said, depending on the initials to give me more to talk about. "His name's Jens, Jens Albert, but everybody calls him—"

"Bert," the man said, and looked up at me for the first time.

I had also been depending on the fact that he would not know my uncle.

"Ya, I know Bert," he said, looking me square in the eye. "He lives south of Standard."

"Exactly," I said, faltering a little. "We're just coming from Drum—I was told there was a shortcut cross-country through Hussar, here someplace…"

"A shortcut?" the man said, rising.

"Well, cross-country," I said, "through the valley, take in the scenery, but…" I felt unconvincing.

The man glanced at the car, then sized me up, still holding the tire iron in a greasy paw.

"Just what the hell are you up to?" he asked suspiciously.

"Me?" I said innocently, but I could feel my smile fading.

The farmer frowned and turned his gaze in the direction of the pasture, but I dodged in front of him. "I guess we missed the road to Hussar?" I said hopefully.

The farmer stepped quickly to the side and I saw his eyes widen before I too turned to take in the view.

The horse hadn't so much as flicked an ear from the last time I'd seen it, while the two old fellows making the beer delivery tiptoed in plain sight about halfway between the back of the barn and the cottonwood tree.

"Hey!" the tee-totaller yelled and took off in the direction of the pasture with the tire iron raised. The two old fellows froze in their tracks, then nearly ran over each other in a hasty about-face.

Taking their lead, I too decided the jig was up and made for the car in ignominious defeat.

"Hey you!" the farmer bellowed as I ducked into the car.

"Let's get out of here!" I said, but Lynne needed no urging and had the vehicle storming down the driveway in reverse before I could close the door. The dust billowed up in our wake, obscuring my view of the charging tee-totaller and his tire iron.

A ways down the driveway Lynne backed into a field, threw the vehicle into first gear and skidded back out onto the drive in the direction of the coulee. I caught a glimpse of the farmer, who had redirected his charge on the pasture and the two retreating cases of beer. We skidded to a halt at the bottom of the draw and scanned the coulee rim anxiously.

We didn't have to wait long. Within seconds our two partners came plummeting over the edge holding the beer cases aloft as they skidded on their rumps through the prickly cactus and sage.

"Drive!" said the first one, diving into the back seat.

"Wait fer me!" bawled the second as he dove in behind.

Looking back, I could see the tee-totaller framed against the sky on the coulee rim, impotently waving his tire iron and bellering his oaths and dark promises.

"What is it with that guy?" I said, giving voice to my shock and amazement.

"He just don't believe horses should drink!" said the first old guy, still badly out of breath.

"I need a beer!" said the second, wiping a layer of dust and sweat from his wrinkled old brow.

Cold beers seemed to be in order all around, except for Lynne, who mostly just shook her head while scanning the rear-view mirror to see if we were being followed.

Nobody felt like going back to the bar. We dropped our partners off, with the beer, at one of their places up the valley. All agreed that there is no second-guessing fate, and rather than lamenting our joint losses at its hands, we joined together in a final toast to Lawrence and Tinker, and all who had shared the pleasure of their company in days gone by—but never forgotten.

Smokey in Wonderland

"A real horse?" asked Benny Timms.

"Of course," said Roland Wright, the director, "and a pig."

"...and a pig," Benny echoed, his eyebrows involuntarily rising another notch. Benny was to be the show's stage manager.

In the world of live theatre there seems to exist a certain prejudice against casting animals and children. In the case of the children, this could have more to do with a desire to avoid dealing with the proverbial stage mother (or father) than the child—of course there are the long hours of rehearsal, the late nights of the run and the presumed inexperience. In the case of the animals, one might suppose the bias to stem from a belief in their unwillingness to take direction.

But, there are exceptions, and *Alice in the Park*—the show's title—was one of them. In fact, there were many aspects to *Alice* which would qualify it as exceptional. For one thing it was to be staged without a stage. Instead of seating the audience before a platform on which the scenery would change as the story unfolded, the scenes would be hidden at various locations in the park, which occupied a creek valley in the city's core. The audience, taking its cue from the White Rabbit or Alice, would follow the action on foot, discovering in this tree the Cheshire Cat; in that hidden glen the Mad Tea Party; and continue on from scene to scene.

Or such was the theory; a theory which Benny Timms, the stage manager—minus a stage—still seemed to be grappling with.

"I don't remember a horse in *Alice in Wonderland*!?"

"We had to invent him," said the director, leaning over a crude map of the location on the table before them.

"Look, the play starts here at this grove of trees next to the parking lot. The White Rabbit pops down his hole, which turns into a tunnel, which leads through the trees to Tweedle Dee and Tweedle Dum standing on the other side of the grove, next to the giant mushroom. The Tweedles eventually inform Alice (and therefore the audience) that the White Rabbit was last seen headed across this field, in the direction of that grove of trees to the south—which houses the Tea Party here, Pig and Pepper here, the Queen's Court here, and so on…"

"And so…?" said Benny, staring at the map and clinging, in his imagination, to what he remembered of the actual layout of the park.

"So," said Roland, "we're pretty sure the kids will follow Alice and the Rabbit through the tunnel as far as the Tweedles; and, on the other side of the field, the locations are close enough to each other that when one scene ends they'll hear the next one start up and go looking for it. So, our problem is to get them across the field without taking forever, or without having them wandering off in all directions and forgetting what they're doing in the park in the first place."

"And so the horse?" prompted Benny.

"And so we've invented a character called the 'Black and White Knight of Day' to chase 'em across the field on horseback!" The director seemed quite pleased with himself.

"Chase them?" Benny asked, as if he hadn't heard correctly.

"You bet," said the director confidently. "Decked out in full armour, lance and everything!"

"On a real horse?"

"Of course," said Roland Wright.

"You're going to have a knight in full armour chasing children through the park on horseback with a lance?"

"The Black and White Knight of Day, to be specific," confirmed the director.

"And you don't think anyone among the ticket-buying public might be inclined to object to that?" asked the stage manager.

"Why should they?" Roland said. "I mean, it's not like we're actually going to be running them down or anything."

"I'm relieved to hear that," said Benny. "But how do you plan to guarantee that exactly?"

"It's an illusion; it's theatre!" said the director. "He won't actually come within a country mile of the last straggler."

Benny seemed unconvinced.

"Look," said Roland. "The Tweedles will get the kids out into the field, warning them to watch out for the dread Knight, who is cued to start way over here beyond the brow of this hill." Roland pointed to the spot on the map. "When he comes into view, the Tweedles start screaming 'Run for your lives!' etc., and with Alice in the lead, the kids will naturally take off for the bush to the south—I mean, obviously they're not going to run for the Knight."

"Some might," interjected Benny.

"Mob hysteria will rule," Roland reassured him. "And the horse canters toward them until he's maybe halfway across the field—by which time most of the kids will have made it to the bush—then he slowly veers off out of sight around the far side of the grove. They hear the Tea Party in progress, and come sneaking out of the bush (with Alice) and we're into the next scene—the horse won't even come close to catching up to them; they'll only believe it will. That's theatre," said the director.

"A stick horse would be theatre," said Benny. "A real horse is real."

"Kids don't care," said the director. "You could have a hundred of the little monsters in that field—some guy comes over that hill with a stick between his legs waving a lance at them—he might just end up needing the armour, if not the lance!"

"And the pig?" Benny asked.

"Same thing," said Roland. "When Alice peeks into the bassinet to get a look at the Duchess' baby and says 'It's a Pig' it's gotta be a real pig!"

Benny sighed deeply as if resigning himself to a world in which directors direct, and stage managers manage.

Auditions had gone well. Of course, no director is ever completely satisfied. In this case, Roland Wright may have wished for a somewhat younger Alice. The actress in question was probably in her early thirties and with a somewhat gravelly voice due, in part, to the roll-yer-own cigarettes that she tended to chain-smoke when not on stage. But, she was petite, and she could act—which put her well ahead of most of the others vying for the role.

Tweedle Dee and Tweedle Dum turned out rather gaunt and lean, but well matched. Tweedle Dum, it turned out, tippled, so that over the weeks of rehearsals the pair came to be known affectionately as Tweedle Dee and Tweedle Drunk—an exaggeration, the director told himself, and besides, the Tweedles were never expected to make a lot of sense anyway.

The Duchess, it was decided, would be played by a man: a man who did an entirely aristocratic lady reeking of superiority—and diesel fuel if he had not had time to make it home to change between work and rehearsals. He drove a fuel delivery truck during the day.

The Cheshire Cat was to be played by a rather stunning—one might even say voluptuous—young woman whose costume did nothing to take away from this. The total effect was probably the most seductively feline version of the character ever played.

They were fortunate enough to cast a veteran actress quite well known in the city who would be taking on the role of the Queen of Hearts. When this woman bawled "Off with her head!" there was no doubt her order would be followed.

The White Rabbit was hyperactive, on and off the stage; the Dormouse vague; the Mad Hatter obtuse. All in all, quite a creditable gathering of Lewis Carroll's hallucinations in the flesh, thought Roland Wright. In his down moments, he consoled himself with thoughts of Yvonne, the costume mistress, who was undeniably brilliant and could be counted on to save the illusion come what may.

Roland had sought out another veteran actor quite well known locally—but more for his personal eccentricities—in hopes that he could be convinced to don the armor of the Black and White Knight of Day. Although getting up in years, he was still vigorous and quite game. He had learned to ride in India as a young doctor in the British military. Though once quite active in the local Little Theatre group, playing roles such as Henry Higgins in *My Fair Lady*, it had been some years since the man had last ventured onto the stage.

"It's the lines, you see—bloody hard work—people don't realize . . ." said Torquhil Matheson to Roland Wright, director.

"But you wouldn't have any lines," said Roland.

"What? What was that—sorry…," said Matheson, cupping a hand over his right ear and inclining it in Roland's direction. "My hearing isn't what it used to be."

"I say," said Roland loudly, "you wouldn't have to worry about memorizing lines."

"Not memorize the lines?" retorted Matheson. "Do you mean carry the book on stage? That sort of thing? Well, I suppose if everyone was doing it…"

"No, sorry," Roland interjected. "What I mean is, you wouldn't have any lines!"

Matheson straightened himself and looked at Roland Wright. There may have been a slight flicker of disappointment showing in the elder man's eyes. "Short of spear carriers, are you?" he said.

"Well," said Roland, more or less to himself, "one lance carrier anyway."

"What? What was that?" said Matheson, once more inclining an ear in Roland's direction.

"Sorry," said Roland. "I say we need a lance carrier actually—we need someone to play the part of a Knight—you'll ride horseback in a full suit of armour—the part's actually pivotal to the action."

"Did you say horseback?" asked Matheson, not fully trusting his ears.

"That's right," confirmed Roland. "The character's called the Black and White Knight of Day."

"And you actually propose to have me ride horseback onto the stage?" Matheson now seemed quite intrigued.

"It's an outdoor play—we're doing it down in the park," said the director.

"Ahh, I see, I see—yes of course, outdoors, it would be—yes, well it sounds quite fun, actually," said the Black and White Knight of Day.

With that, the cast was complete—except, of course, for the two four-legged members of the troupe, namely the Horse and the Pig.

Quite early on in the rehearsal schedule, the director had put the word out to all cast members, asking them to pass on the names of anyone who might help them locate the Duchess' baby and the Knight's trusty steed.

Tweedle-Drunk, or rather Dum, had come forward to say that he owned an old horse that would be perfect! He kept it on his brother's farm east of the city. He'd also informed them that his brother kept pigs, and would, no doubt, be happy to lend them one for the play.

"I'll phone him," said the tippling Tweedle. "I'll tell 'im you want to take the old plug for a ride."

Early one afternoon in the final week before the Saturday opening, Roland Wright and Benny Timms sallied forth into the country.

Having located what they believed to be the right place, they emerged from the vehicle to be greeted by a man who bore a distinct family resemblance to the Tweedle who had sent them.

Introductions were made, and Roland Wright in due course reviewed the purpose of their visit. There was a pause as the man looked them over, then suddenly broke out laughing.

The director and the stage manager exchanged glances.

"Didn't your brother explain what we wanted?" asked Roland plaintively.

"I didn't think he was serious," said the brother, and laughed again. "That's his horse over there," he said, bringing the proceedings to order.

Wright and Timms looked in the direction indicated to see a smoky grey buckskin standing in the shade of the barn.

"He is perfect!" said the director, moving spontaneously in the direction of the horse. "What's he like around children?"

"Oh, I suppose he'd be all right—depends on what you want 'im to do, I guess."

"Chase them!" said Benny.

"What?" said the farmer.

"He's kidding," said Roland, leaning on the fence. "He certainly looks quiet enough."

"Oh, he's quiet, all right. Our kids crawl all over him, and under him—he's never bothered."

"He's perfect!" the director said again. "Your brother said you have some pigs."

"All kinds of 'em," said the farmer with a shrug. "They're out back."

On the way through the barn, they made the acquaintance of the farmer's little girl who, the director couldn't help thinking, would have made a perfect Alice. He told her so.

"My name's Narda," she said.

Moments later, the party stood silently surveying a series of pig pens, the occupants of which seemed to average around two hundred pounds each.

"They're awfully big," said the director.

"Well, they're pigs," said the farmer matter-of-factly.

"You don't have anything smaller?" asked Roland.

"Well…" The man paused to scratch his head.

"Is it going to be in the play?" asked Narda.

"Yes, it plays the part of a baby," said Benny Timms.

"They could use Bettina," the girl said quietly.

"Who?" asked the director.

"Oh, she's kinda made a pet outa one of 'em," answered the father.

Back at the barn, the men stared in wonder at the blonde little girl cradling a coal-black pig, which responded by nuzzling the girl under the chin.

"You can only hold her upside down like this if you rub her tummy," Narda explained quietly.

The men couldn't believe their luck! Even Benny was starting to believe in animals.

"She's wonderful!" exclaimed Roland.

Narda smiled shyly, gently rocking Bettina who responded with a sigh while, apparently, drifting off to sleep.

"We're set!" enthused the director as they drove back to town. The stage manager nodded in silent agreement. In due course arrangements were made to have the animals delivered to the dress rehearsal, which would take place on the Friday evening before opening day. Tickets were being made available to the farmer for any and all of the shows his family would care to attend.

Rehearsing the dialogue of the various little scenes had been relatively easy. It was the transitional bits between which, in the absence of the audience, had presented something of a vacuum of speech.

"Just be your character and ad lib whatever comes to mind," the director had told them.

When they arrived on the Friday, Smokey and Bettina had created something of a sensation among the cast and crew. Smokey took it in stride, but Bettina seemed to display a somewhat temperamental disposition and squealed loudly whenever anyone tried to lift her off the ground.

"Rub its belly," directed Roland Wright.

Of course Smokey had Tweedle Dum to introduce him to the group, and to the Black and White Knight of Day in particular, who was soon in the saddle and romping up and down the park as if he'd been doing it all his life.

Yvonne, true to her reputation, showed up with a complete suit of armour, including a helmet and visor for the Knight errant and a face guard and skirting for the Steed.

"It's only a replica," she said, half apologetically. "I made the horsey bits out of papier mâché."

"It's magnificent!" declared the director—and it was.

They walked through the scenes in turn until coming to the crossing of the field. Here they paused to load the Knight onto his charger—a job which required some effort once he was ensconced in the armour—and spotted him out of sight behind the hill.

Since verbal cues were out—bringing him on with shouts and yells would detract from the illusion—a relay of visual clues had to be arranged.

The director had the cast and crew stand in for the audience, whereupon the Tweedles led them out into the field, cowering all the way.

"I don't believe there is any such thing as a Black and White Knight of Day," ad libbed Alice.

Roland waved back to Benny who flagged Torquhil and, lo, over the rise came the Knight!

"Run for your lives!" sang Tweedle Dee.

"Verily!" sang Tweedle Drunk, and everybody did!

Over the field they went, fleeing before the very real menace of the Knight brandishing his lance and bellowing "Gallumph! Gallumph!" (Torquhil having decided he should have at least one line) as they came.

As the cast made the safety of the trees, the horse and rider veered off in a gentle arc, like a shark circling a bay, and disappeared around the far side of the grove of trees.

"Perfect!" shouted the director, calling the company back. "Excellent! It's going to work like a dream!"

All applauded as Smokey walked up to join the circle.

"Do it just like that!" said the director, as happy as directors can be.

"Bloody good horse this," said the Knight, patting the neck of the steady beast.

They finished the run without incident and set about the task of packing up the props, set pieces and costumes—like a circus getting ready to move on—for the night.

"Set-up time tomorrow is ten o'clock," Benny called out to the assembled personnel. "All cast here by noon; the show goes up at two o'clock sharp!"

With that the company began to break up.

"Where is Smokey staying?" asked Torquhil as he held the animal on a lead line letting it graze.

The stage manager looked at the director who looked to Tweedle Dum. "I live in an apartment," he said, "an' I don't think they allow pets."

"Damn," said the director. "Never thought of this."

"Not to worry," said Matheson. "He shall stay with me!"

"With you?" said Benny.

"Our back garden is fenced all around—just have to lay in some sort of barrier in the breezeway."

"Are you sure?" asked Roland.

"Absolutely!" said Torquhil.

"Here," he added, tossing Benny his car keys and making ready to mount up. "Bring the car around, will you?"

And they were off.

Alice, who had fallen in love instantly with Bettina, declared that her daughter's rabbit had died, leaving a vacancy at their place. The pig could stay in the old hutch overnight.

"Perfect!" declared Roland Wright.

Benny thought a production meeting might be in order to see what else they may not have thought of. Roland agreed, and they planned to reconvene at his place. Dropping by Torquhil's to drop off his car, they found him busily packing ladders, wheelbarrow, lawn mower and all manner of things into the breezeway.

"Just tie him up!" suggested Roland.

"Better to let him graze—take but a minute—best this way," said Matheson.

"All right," said the director with a shrug.

"See you tomorrow," said Benny as they pulled away.

"Cheerio!" called the white-haired gentleman with a wave.

It was late by the time Roland and Benny had satisfied themselves that their work was done. They were just about to adjourn for the night when the phone rang.

It was Torquhil. "Gone!" he said.

"What?" said Roland.

"The horse, I'm afraid, escaped!"

"Are you sure?" said Roland.

"Quite," said Matheson. "It is a horse, after all—quite hard to miss really."

"We'll be right over," said Roland and hung up.

When they stepped outside, the director and stage manager were further chagrined to find out it was raining.

"Perfect!" said the director bitterly.

"Nothing I can do about the rain," said the stage manager.

Minutes later they were at Matheson's. The man met them in the driveway dressed in a slicker and tall rubber boots, and climbed into the back seat, bridle in hand.

"Phoned the police and radio station," he said. "A man phoned in from the petrol station on 100th Avenue, says he saw a horse go by headed east a half-hour ago."

"He's headed home," said Benny.

And so he was. The men drove the back roads, tramped the fields and slogged through bush for two hours before almost falling over him in a spruce meadow where he had decided to bed down—or hide out—for the night.

"I'll ride 'im back," said Benny, resigned to his fate.

"Not at all," said Matheson. "My blunder. I'm dressed for it, after all! Just give us a leg up, will you…" Roland did.

"I left the brandy out on the table—the good brandy, mind you," said the Knight, gathering up the reins. "You two go on ahead and make sure there's lots of hot water on the boil when I get there. Cheerio!"

The stage manager and the director were well into their third hot brandy before the Knight, having tied up his untrustworthy steed in the back yard, joined them. They celebrated Smokey's capture, and lamented their prospects for tomorrow now drowning in the rain…and finally went their separate ways to sleep.

But the morning dawned to brilliant sunshine. The company, giddy with expectation, set about their various tasks until by one-thirty all were in costume and bunkered down in their separate locations awaiting an audience. It was strange not to be together backstage listening to the public slowly file in.

Out front, at the parking lot, the director and stage manager were gratified to see a modest line-up begin to form before the crude stand that served as a box office.

Alice sat on the lawn between the parking lot and the grove of trees chatting, as one, with the growing circle of kids. The adults tended to hang back, observing.

As a last-minute contingency, Roland had donned the costume of a Herald and carried a bugle under his arm. Should the audience not "get" that they should move on cue, he would be able to direct them as a sort of town crier. He might have spared himself the effort.

Around two he gave a sign to the stage manager that it was time to begin, and Benny sidled off through the crowd. Moments later the White Rabbit was in their midst, too late to say hello but saying goodbye to all he met—darting here, stopping there, agitating everywhere—until he suddenly popped down a hole and disappeared!

For a second or two, the children gazed after him as if expecting to see him pop back. Then, suddenly deciding he would not, and before Alice could lead the way, they began diving into the hole after the Rabbit. Indeed, Alice realized with a start that she had to act fast or she'd be bringing up the rear!

Some of the adults braved the tunnel while others—obviously including those with strollers, stood gaping after the disappearing mob at a complete loss as to what they should do next.

"You may come this way if you like," said the director/Herald, and led the way around the grove of trees to where Tweedle Dee and Tweedle Dum were engaging Alice and the growing mob of her peers emerging from the tunnel in "Tweedle Banter." Roland estimated the audience to be around one hundred and twenty in all.

Eventually Alice got around to asking which way the White Rabbit had gone.

"That way!" said Tweedle Dee, indicating south.

"This way!" said Tweedle Dum, and began bumping through the crowd of kids into the field.

"I don't see him," said Alice.

"You can't," said Tweedle Dee.

"Verily," said Tweedle Dum.

"Nonsense," said Alice. "I saw him quite plainly only a moment ago!"

"I mean," said Tweedle Dee, "he disappeared."

"Into those trees over there," added Tweedle Dum.

"Then we must go find him," said Alice, and the mob around her added their own demands to that effect.

"We can't," said Tweedle Dee.

"Impossible!" said Tweedle Dum.

"Why?" demanded Alice, whereupon the Tweedles began bewailing the dangers of being caught out in the open at the mercy of the Black and White Knight of Day!

"I don't believe there's any such thing!" the brave little Alice declared.

"Oh yes there is!" said Tweedle Dee.

"Verily!" said Tweedle Dum emphatically.

Roland, bringing up the rear with his brigade of strollers, was so caught up in the controversy that he very nearly forgot to cue Benny.

"And there he is!" shouted Tweedle Dee, pointing across the field to the brow of the hill where the woeful countenance of the Knight had begun to appear.

"Verily!" added Tweedle Dum as the children went suddenly quiet.

"Run for your lives!" screamed Tweedle Dee.

"Verraleeee!" screamed Dum and set the example by bolting for the trees.

The mob screamed and soon passed them both—except for the parents and strollers who paused to admire the novel spectacle of a Knight on horseback, steadily cantering towards them.

"Hurry!" yelled the director/Herald and began alternately jogging toward the trees and dropping back to assist the more sluggardly strollers. He was gratified to see a look of fear on more than one face as the adults, glancing over their shoulders, leaned into their efforts to make the safety of the trees.

On came the dread Knight—and on…and on…and on?

Roland now glanced back with his own look of fear. Why wasn't he veering off?

On came the Knight, apparently drawing a bead on the harried band of stragglers, most of the children having long since made the safety of the tree line. And still on…

Roland, looking back once again, was horrified to see that the visor of the helmet had apparently fallen down over the Black and White Knight's eyes! With his lance in his right hand, he had been forced to drop the reins onto the horse's neck and was madly pushing, pulling and pounding on the offending visor and helmet with his left! To no avail!

There was a narrow trail leading through the dense hedge into the clearing where the Dormouse, Mad Hatter and White Rabbit waited to commence the Mad Tea Party.

Smokey, having been given no other direction, was obviously headed down this trail. The stragglers hurriedly parted to let him pass. Roland, looking ahead now, almost screamed himself as he spied a young lady attempting to push her tandem stroller—bearing her identical twins—over the sandy path.

"Look out!" he yelled, and the young mother looked back only to freeze in terror. At the last minute, and just when it seemed the horse was deciding to jump over the twins, Tweedle Dum streaked out of the hedge and swept the stroller and mother to one side.

On went the Knight, still fighting with his head-gear, now directly at the Mad Tea Party laid out at the table set a distance into the clearing at the head of the path! Here the horse veered sharply to avoid the table (and actors), unbalancing the Knight who dropped the point of his lance while attempting to right himself. The lance drove into the turf next to the table, jogging the man back upright in the saddle, and horse and rider plunged on to disappear out the other side of the glen.

Slowly, the actors emerged from under the table to gaze after the sounds of brush breaking in the distance.

"Good grief!" said the Mad Hatter, genuinely perturbed.

"No room?" prompted Alice tenuously from the sidelines.

The kids were glowing with excitement. Roland thought he heard a pig squeal.

"No room!" shouted the Mad Hatter, echoed by the Dormouse still glancing over his shoulder as if fearing that the Knight might suddenly return to retrieve his lance.

The audience too crept into the clearing cautiously, as the scene slowly came to life.

Roland, the director, wasn't hearing a word. When he wasn't replaying the preceding scene in his mind, horrified all over again at what might have happened, he was trying to imagine what was happening with horse and rider at the moment.

Suddenly he became aware that the White Rabbit had once again bolted and Alice, and the audience, were once again off in search of him. Roland followed along.

"Who are you?" demanded a voice overhead. The assembly gazed up into a massive poplar tree where a giant, and very female, cat lounged languidly on an overhanging limb.

"Who are you?" countered Alice.

"I'm not who I seem," said the cat.

"I didn't ask you who you're not," said Alice.

"You're the Cheshire Cat!" said one of the children boldly.

"Mmmm," purred the cat, gazing down upon the child. "You're cute."

You're enchanting, observed the director to himself. But where, he wondered, did poor Torquhil end up?

The Cat sent them on to the Duchess. The kids gambolled eagerly on ahead following the sounds of violent sneezing, to discover its source: the cook, flailing away with the pepper shaker while the Duchess glared. Something didn't seem right. Alice shyly drew closer until she was close enough to peek into the bassinet—then suddenly seemed to freeze.

"It's not a pig!" said the Duchess, and glared at Roland for some reason he couldn't quite comprehend.

"Nooo…," ad libbed Alice somewhat poorly, then recovered slightly with, "It's not anything at all!"

"Correct!" barked the Duchess fiercely.

They gradually resurrected enough of the scene to move the audience in the direction of the Queen's Court.

Roland hung back and fell in beside the Duchess at the rear of the pack.

"What happened?" he asked the scowling fuel truck driver.

"That damned horse," said the Duchess in a low voice, "came pounding in and knocked over the bassinet!"

"Where's the pig?"

The Duchess gave a shrug. "It hit the ground and took off running like its tail was on fire!"

"And the horse?"

The Duchess shrugged again. "Just kept on going, I guess?"

As they entered the court, the White Rabbit was cowering before the Queen of Hearts. "Yes, your Majesty, of course…"

"Get on with it then," said the Queen coldly.

"Well," said the Rabbit, and cleared his throat.

"The Queen of Hearts,
She made some tarts,
All on a summer's day.
This Alice girl
With flaxen curls,
She stole the tarts away!"

"I did no such thing!" said Alice, aghast.

"Mind your manners, girl!" the Queen warned.

"My manners? Why I've never been treated so rudely in all my life!"

"That's quite enough!" declared the Queen, then glowering at Alice added, "Apologize at once!"

"I will not!"

"Then," said the Queen menacingly, "either you or your head must be off immediately!"

"That's the most ridiculous thing I've ever heard," declared Alice. "Why you're behaving more like a clown than a Queen!"

The entire court gasped in fearful expectation of what must surely follow. The Queen slowly drew herself up to full height.

"Off—"

But she was cut off by a collective scream from the children before she could finish her line. They began running pell-mell through the court and through the hedge on its northern boundary. Roland glanced up to see Torquhil, finally free of his helmet, trotting into the court from the south.

"Is it over?" he asked, seeming unsure.

"It is now," said the Duchess.

"Off with his head," said the Queen sourly as the last of the audience trickled past.

"Bad show that," said the Knight, dismounting. "This blasted helmet—couldn't see a blasted thing!"

Roland Wright, the director, slowly sat down as many of the children—having discovered that there was nothing on the other side of the hedge but their parents waiting to take them home, filtered back into the court to mix with the cast. A large group of them were pressed tightly around Smokey and Torquhil, who was answering their questions concerning knights and armour and horses. Smokey had lifted a hind foot and was now gingerly feeling around for some place to set it down that didn't have a child under it.

"Has anyone seen the pig?" Roland asked listlessly.

"They're still looking," answered Benny Timms.

The Game
of Polo

*P*olo, the sport of kings, millionaires and film stars. Could it be played by run-of-the-mill Canadians selected at random from among the great unwashed? This was the question the events of the day would decide.

The idea had had its genesis, as these things often do, with one man. Cledwyn Lewis had studied polo as a doctor in the British Army. Since then he'd gone on to play on several continents, upholding the very best traditions of his motherland. (Technically, Cledwyn was Welsh, but to the untrained ears and eyes of the average Canadian cowboy, he came across as "just another Englishman.")

When fate and life's ever-changing fortunes had seen fit to plunk the man down in the unkempt reaches of northwestern Alberta, Cled had not taken long in applying "Cledwyn's Law," which reads: "When in Rome, the Romans shall play polo!"

Over the days of spring and into the early summer, he had scurried about inviting, cajoling and press-ganging patients, colleagues, the postman and generally anyone who had a horse into taking up the game of polo. For a polo field, he had commandeered a cow pasture from his friend James and the small group of friends who lived on the farm.

It was James who had been instrumental in selecting a local purveyor of horseflesh from whom Cledwyn was to procure his first Canadian mount. Calls were made and on a sunny Sunday afternoon James and Cled mounted a rickety-looking staircase and knocked on the door of the revered and rugged Jonas H. Webber.

Mr. Webber made a living at, among other things, buying, breaking and selling horses. His age, somewhere around eighty, seemed to be no impediment to him—indeed the strength and agility of his body seemed only to be outdone by the strength and obvious agility of his mind.

However, on this occasion, it was Mrs. Webber who greeted them at the door and bade them enter, a profound look of woe pervading her usually pleasant and generally cordial features.

"He's in here," she said softly, and led them into the living room.

There, fully dressed in his vest, buckle, cowboy boots and pink shirt, lay Mr. Webber stretched out upon the chesterfield with his hands folded upon his chest.

"Come in," he said without moving his head to view the men. A rasping gurgle deep in his chest gradually turned into a rasping cough followed by an obviously painful effort to gather up and expectorate the offending clot of blood into a saucepan on the floor near his head.

"It was my own fault," he said, as he relaxed back onto the couch. "I wasn't watching."

Then, methodically, in his clipped and characteristic manner, he went on to explain how, while feeding the horses, he had walked out among them to spread a bale. One horse had taken a bite out of another horse. That horse had reared off blind and caught the unwary Mr. Webber full in the chest with both its knees.

Mrs. Webber arrived with the coffee as Mr. Webber, having finished the story, expelled another clot of blood into the pan at his side.

Unable to ignore the obvious, Cled cautiously explained that he was a doctor and then, in a sincere and almost humble tone, opined, "Mr. Webber, I believe you may have some internal injuries."

For the first time, and ignoring the obvious discomfort it caused him, Mr. Webber turned to face his visitor. He stared at Cled for a long enquiring moment, then, lying back with an involuntary groan, answered, "You don't say."

Not one to let his pride stand in the way of a patient's welfare, Cled rejoined, "Yes, I do, and I think perhaps you may want to consult your doctor about it."

Webber, picking up on Cled's obvious sincerity, cleared his throat again and gave the two men his personal assessment of the options that he felt he had.

"When it comes to doctoring," he began, "yes, I could, at considerable inconvenience to myself, have Mrs. Webber drive me into Beaverlodge and up to the hospital. A doctor could then, at a cost of some further pain and inconvenience to myself, poke and prod, X-ray and cross-examine in between my visits to the waiting room, until, in the end, I would be told that there was 'a possibility' that I had some internal injuries and that what I needed was complete rest while the body repaired itself!"

Conceding the possibility, Cled let the whole thing drop and, in order to facilitate the injured man's rest, they got right down to brass tacks.

Before getting hit, the horse-trader had corralled a young Appaloosa, his pick for the purpose at hand. The men strode out to view the first potential polo pony of the Peace Country.

He was pretty enough. The men leaned on the rails and eyed the young horse as he paced up and down the opposite side of the corral.

They went back to the house to ask Mr. Webber if the horse would buck, balk or glide, given the rigours of the ancient game he was supposed to learn.

"No, he wouldn't buck," said the old wrangler indignantly. "Unless you went to work and drove him to it; then I suppose he would buck just fine," he added.

It wasn't the prospect of being bucked off that flashed before Cled's eyes so much as the resulting waste of precious time. He had no desire to spend the few free hours he so jealously guarded convincing unwilling partners of the four-legged kind that they wanted to play polo. Willing, or at least submissive, members of the equine race could be bought, which was what Cledwyn had in mind.

He had explained it poorly. James, who had known Mr. Webber for some time, saw the shift in the old horse-trader's eyes from the propitious to the punitive.

"Well, there is one horse that might be what you're looking for," surmised Mr. Webber. "It might be a little kid spoiled, but it's guaranteed not to buck." He was actually selling him for a neighbour down the way and thought he could get him at a pretty fair price.

"An amazing price, at least," thought James when he heard it, but kept his thoughts to himself as he watched Cledwyn talk himself into the leap.

When they left the Webbers', the men drove down to the neighbour's to view the prospective steed.

He stood alone on the far side of the pasture against the tree line. They crossed the fence and walked out into the pasture to "count his legs" and ascertain whether or not he might be inclined to play the sport of kings.

As the men approached, the horse seemed to regard them with as much interest and curiosity as he would two more flies buzzing tediously around his head. James did not immediately cotton to the rather pluggish-looking old fellow, but something in the animal's stationary ways seemed to catch his eye.

"He'll be easy to catch," said Cledwyn enthusiastically, obviously thinking once again about future savings in time.

So it was that "Socks" (so dubbed by Cled's children after his four white fetlocks—the rest of him was a dirty grey) became the first polo pony in the Peace!

It was also arranged that Socks was to be a guest at James' farm, working off his board trail riding before his illustrious debut in "the big match," scheduled some weeks hence. Cledwyn was to be out of the country until then.

In the ensuing weeks, James was to discover that when Jonas had said "kid spoiled," he had been referring to the horse's rather annoying habit of quietly seeking out low-hanging limbs or barbed-wire fences with which to swipe off, or rub off, unsuspecting passengers. Slyly selecting a limb within reach, Socks would take the bit firmly between his teeth and lean into the potential "rider-remover" with grim and unerring accuracy.

Someone, either unwilling or unable to correct the horse of this innovative tendency, had put up with it until the habit had become a feature of the animal's makeup.

Neither had James drawn the line and taken the time to work this out of him. He had horses of his own that needed "schooling."

Still, on the morning of the big day, as he headed down to the barn to start getting ready, he wished he'd taken the time. Cledwyn would be arriving any minute for a "test drive."

The barnyard was a sea of mud. Steady rains had threatened to flood the old log barn. Before its gaping doorway, a boggy puddle had steadily grown into a swampy lake.

James, leading Socks and his own saddle horse out of the gloomy interior of the barn, jumped to the side, skittering along on the grass that grew at the base of the barn and beneath the rails of the corral. He cursed when he caught the splatter from the horses' feet as they splashed through the muddy water.

Tying them to the corral adjacent to the barn door, he then went about brushing, saddling and tacking up the pair. Just as he was beginning to wonder what was keeping Socks' master, the familiar station wagon roared into the barnyard and up to the gate.

The Cledwyn that emerged, however, was not nearly so familiar. He was wearing riding boots, knee-high and polished to within an inch of the bootblack's life, and white, in fact dazzling white, jodhpurs and polo shirt.

"How are you lad—good to see you," said the Welshman, striding forth, hand outstretched and a familiar smile upon his face.

"Fine," said James, forcing himself out of the trance-like state his mind had wandered into, attempting to grasp the significance of Cled's pristine apparel.

"Ahh…," said Cledwyn, sucking up a lungful of barnyard, summer, sunshine and the general feeling that for the next few hours he was to be truly free. "It's a great day!"

With that he entered the corral, stepping gingerly along on the grass at its edge. He untied Socks' halter shank and was making ready to board the steady beast when the opportune nature of the circumstances caught James' eye.

"Ahh, ya better watch that pig," James said, forgetting for a moment whose horse it was. "He'll probably try to swipe you off on the barn door." (To exit the corral, it would be necessary for Cled to turn directly in front of the cave-like entrance.)

"Oh he will, will he?" asked the plucky Welshman as he mounted the horse.

"All right Socks!" he said, and pulling the horse's head around, gave him a curt slap on the rump with his braided leather riding crop (an item James thought made a very appropriate accessory to Cled's dazzling outfit).

For a moment it looked as though the horse was going to head dutifully out to the pasture, but, as the opening in the wall of the barn passed before its panning gaze, James could see the thought pop into its all too predictable brain.

Before he could speak, Socks had veered off in long even strides—despite considerable threats and oaths from Cledwyn. With the bit clenched iron-jawed between his yellow teeth, Socks walked through the open door at a steady, purposeful pace.

The saddle horn barely grazed the top of the opening as they cruised by. Cledwyn, bracing his hands against the logs above the door, slid back over the cantle and onto the horse's rump.

Socks never paused, but continued on his plodding way into the dark recesses of the barn. Here things took a turn for the dangerous. Cled, now clinging to the top of the door, had failed to release either polished boot from the stirrups that were now pulling up along the horse's sides.

Socks didn't bat an eye but strained on with his wet hooves slipping on the barn floor while his rider became stretched out between the lintel and stirrups. Cled's grip was giving way and he was about to fall dangerously over the horse's hindquarters.

But the stirrups suddenly gave up their grip, catapulting Cledwyn, white jodhpurs and all, into the lake in front of the door. For a moment, James lost sight of him in the spume and spray, but in the next second he reappeared, gasping for air midst the ooze and the slime and doing a sort of frantic dog-paddle in an attempt to get upright again.

"That &%$#*&!" he cursed, standing in the centre of the mud-hole and staring, hands on hips, into the black abyss of the barn.

Deaf to James' laughter, as well as his suggestion that Cled go for a rinse in the water trough, the "polo player from the black lagoon" splashed through the mudhole and disappeared into the barn.

He reappeared moments later, leading the ever-placid Socks, midst much cursing and slapping, slipping and spitting.

In the centre of the corral, in all his earthen glory, Cled climbed aboard the animal, daring him to even consider such tricky manoeuvres again, and rode out to inspect the polo pitch/cow pasture.

Early in the afternoon, the first of the motley mob of recruits began to arrive. The Frenchman from just down the way rode in on a well-lathered Shetland pony–Arabian cross (or so he said; James always had trouble seeing the Arabian). The Frenchman, however, had all the confidence in the world in the diminutive beast and fully intended to play away the entire afternoon on it.

The fellow's wife arrived in their battered old pickup truck. She didn't pull a trailer, but instead hauled, directly in the box of her truck, the most elephantine Quarterhorse anyone present had ever seen. This, just to offer the ridiculous a glimpse of the sublime, was her chosen mount. One couldn't help wondering what debates had taken place over the relative merits of the two animals. It soon became apparent that the day's match would see the discussion carried onto the field in a sort of "we'll see" grudge match between the two riders.

Next came Cled's lawyer, driving a chrome-encrusted pickup with a four-horse trailer of professional proportions behind. However, when the back doors of the trailer were opened, the lawyer led out a single rather tired-looking sorrel, which later was discovered to be blind in one eye.

A one-ton truck was next, loaded with about two-and-a-half tons of mustangs (bought from the Indians at Nose Creek). Their new owner lost no time in dumping them into the corral and sorting through them to see which would like to play polo—and which would rather die.

James lost track of "who" and "how many" as the place fairly leapt to life. Many people who didn't happen to bring a horse, or perhaps had never ridden a horse, were still game, anxious even, to give the sport a try.

Cled doled out sticks (five-foot lengths of bamboo or fibreglass with a wedge of hardwood on the end) and balls to all comers.

Soon, sticks were swinging, horses were rearing and balls were flying in and out of every corner of the crowded little farmstead. When this general mayhem had about reached its peak, Cled mounted up and led a mass exodus—cars, bars, trucks, bales of hay, a gang of kids and a growing pack of barking dogs—out to the cow pasture.

Down at one end, at the edge of the slough, a couple of bales were set out as a goal. At the other end, a prudent ten or fifteen feet out from a barbed-wire fence, two more bales (which several spectators availed themselves of as front-row seats) were laid for the opposite goal.

Cled made a short declaration on the rules, of which there seemed to be surprisingly few. (James noticed that Cled did add rules as the game moved along, however.)

Having been successful in cutting the first wave of competitors into two opposing herds, Cledwyn signalled an honoured guest to make the first "toss-in."

The person, on foot, didn't toss it in far enough, however, and was forced to run for his life as the two teams converged.

Most were successful in aiming their mounts in the general direction of the ball. There was a modicum of good-natured jockeying for position as they collided, and a great deal of windmill-like work on the sticks.

One of the horses actually had the temerity and lack of good sense to stand on the yet-to-be-clubbed orb, bringing a shower of hardwood down upon itself and pressing the hard little sphere into the soft earth of the pasture.

Since for one reason and another it had been agreed that a referee would not be necessary, there was no one to whistle down the play. All continued to mill about, some swiping at the half-buried ball, others still attempting to find it.

One fellow, aboard one of the mustangs, had not been successful in joining in the original charge. His horse had first balked, then offered to buck and then took off in a wrong direction. Once he had it straightened out, flat out, he drew a bead on the duffing melee across the field. As they bore down upon it, the rider, sizing up the apparent congestion of traffic around the ball, was hit by a sudden and ingenious inspiration. He began whirling his stick around his head like a cavalry sabre and screaming like an attacking Blackfoot warrior! (While the eyes of his horse rolled back in its head as it ran on all the harder.)

The men in the melee, intent on murdering the little white ball, seemed not to notice the rapidly approaching attacker. Their horses, on the other hand, unanimously agreed that this new player cared nothing for murdering little white balls when horses were in such good supply, and they scattered like chickens.

"No shouting! No shouting!" Cledwyn began screaming, (adding another to the growing list of basic rules) from his seat aboard the ever-placid Socks.

The ball was dug out of the ground and once again tossed into play. Once again, the hordes gathered around, but this time several people were successful in smashing it a good one and gambolling off in pursuit.

Every now and then a sort of rally would break out of the mob, and the whole assembly would be slashing (and splashing) their way pell-mell through the cowpies and rugged turf of the pasture.

Of course, every so often, a horse would revolt, much to the delight of the derisive gang of spectators, and send its rider sprawling or take him on an unscheduled visit back to the barn.

One fellow, "new to horses," had stood up in the stirrups and leaned out over the horse in an effort to reach the ball. Unfortunately, he was using the reins to hold himself on, so when he swung, he inadvertently jerked the horse's head up into his own face, knocking himself over backwards and off the back of the horse.

Apart from two front teeth that now waved back and forth like window shutters, the man wasn't seriously hurt.

The first real injury of the day came in the second period, or "chukka" as Cledwyn called them.

Cled, of course, was quite deft, if a little out of practice, at hitting the ball from the back of a moving horse. (Socks seemed to put up with the stick-handling well; getting him moving was what required the effort.) A handful of others sufficiently at home upon a horse to get into the swing of the game began to pick up the knack very quickly. The second chukka was to be made up of a selection of these and a corresponding number of the least unwilling horses.

Of all people, large and small, the first one damaged turned out to be the most unlikely victim. In fact, one might easily have cast Bull as the one most likely to cause damage. This large hulk of a man had a fiercely competitive enthusiasm, which today he was making a very commendable effort to control.

Bull and James had both made the team, two of the regulation four per side. To be fair, the four deemed to be the best went to this side while Cled took the next three in the line to his.

As the second chukka took off looking like a true game of polo, Cled began to display his own competitiveness. James and Bull were defending the swamp, and Cled, the barbed-wire fence.

James also had the Frenchman who turned out (possibly owing to the fact that on the pony he was the closest to the ground) to be one of the most consistent hitters. The trouble was that, having hit the ball, he would soon be out-distanced in pursuit of it.

Here's where James and Bull would come in. They would dash out on their full-grown horses, one behind the other, and each in turn attempt to move the ball, in one or two hits, towards the goal. With teamwork like this, it wasn't long before the first goal was sizzling through the barbed wire.

Cledwyn, although he was the only one on the field capable of carrying the ball, had to compete with the members of his own team as well as James' for possession. He had not had an opportunity for the all-important breakaway, when James and Bull suddenly did!

The Frenchman had faithfully smacked the ball out of a melee towards the fence. James took off in full pursuit with Bull closing up in the "second-attempt" slot behind. James rose in the saddle, his stick rising like the hand of a giant clock as he closed in on the bouncing ball.

He could feel the bamboo bend and whip as he brought it down for the anticipated "click"—but there was no click. Milliseconds before the hardwood wedge and the ball could connect, the club had connected with something else. As James rode on, he became aware that his partner was not taking his shot and glanced back to see why.

The man was not in the saddle but was clinging perilously by one hand from the saddle horn with one foot up on the cantle. Blood was streaming down the back of his head and neck. Obviously it had been the back of his skull that had connected with the hardwood at the end of James' stick. For reasons he couldn't seem to recall later, the man had hung off the side of his saddle, leaning out with his stick ahead, in an effort to beat James to the shot.

"Cled," James hollered as he rode to catch the horse ahead, now running away with the injured man.

Cled nodded but rode on to where the ball had been left. "I'll just make this shot," he called, and then hammered one out into the middle of the slough before attending to the downed man.

After what seemed to James like a bare minimum of poking and prodding at the hole in the skull, Cled confidently declared that the man would live and turned his attention to resurrecting the fractured chukka.

Bull, when he could finally phrase a complete sentence again, declared that he would be seeking a second opinion, preferably from "a real doctor," at the nearest opportunity. He did stay on to ride in the third and final chukka of the day, however, cheered boisterously on by all, despite the pitiless pounding in his head.

So what, one may ask, did it all prove? Could polo, in all its glory, be played by relatively inglorious men and women? The question was discussed long into the night around the campfire.

"Horses weren't made for that," declared Mr. Webber, now fully recovered. "But they could be adapted," he added, ever conscious of new markets.

Ultimately, all seemed to agree that they had accomplished the one and only thing that matters in a game. For a few mad hours in a cow pasture on the edge of the world, they had all forgotten who the other "was" and had come together as one—just for laughs.

About the Author

If you say the word "story teller" in Grande Prairie, someone is likely to bring up the name Jim Nelson. Jim has been writing about the people and places of Northern Alberta throughout his adult life—and telling the stories from the stage, in both reader's theatre and full theatrical settings. He is best known for his musical theatre explorations—most notably his *Ballad of Knobby Clark* series. Jim's writing credits also include a diversity of film and radio, as in the case of a cowboy poetry series commissioned by the CBC. While his writing has appeared in regional publications and anthologies, this is the first collection of his work to appear in book form.